Guardians of the Cosmic Clocks

The Emerald Tablets

NO. 1

Jabril Yousef Faraj

Table of Contents

For all the little girls (and boys) who are destined to change
the world.

CHAPTER ONE

How Much Is Ever Enough?

As a blood red sun descended over the Nashville evergreens, a little Black girl peered out her second story window, gazing longingly at the horizon. It was the last day of summer and Zya Nicole Jenkins didn't want it to end.

Zya, an old soul in the body of a twelve-year-old, sat on her bed, back arrow-straight with one leg tucked underneath. Staring off into the sky, she mindlessly stroked the coat of her Dachshund-Beagle Hercules. The big, brown egg-of-a-spot over his eye made him look sad most of the time. But Zya knew the truth: he was simply unimpressed.

"Yeah, you and me both," she whispered, scratching him right between the eyes.

Zya was jealous of Herc sometimes. Her calendar was crazy. She was scheduled for something different every night of the week. If it wasn't voice lessons, it was guitar; if it wasn't cheer, she was tagging along to one of her mom's gigs, or babysitting the annoying next-door neighbor. And that was *without* complex fractions. There was always something she had to do. And, yet, somehow, Herc had found a way to be part of the family and still lounge around all day. In fact, it's what he was best at.

Zya, on the other hand, she'd always been a little wild. Well, wilder than most of the other kids, at least. And, sometimes, it got her in a pickle. Like that one time she blew up on Dane after he poked her under the desk the entire class period. And, of course, Mrs. Meyers didn't notice a thing until she struck back. She thought it was quite clever of her — and deserved — to grab his hand and pull so quickly that it caused Dane's head to smack against the desk. Mrs. Meyers disagreed. Somehow, *she* was always the one who got in trouble, even when she was just standing up for herself. As far as Zya was concerned, though, being spunky was less of a problem than a superpower. The only problem was that most people were too blind to see for themselves.

Herc extended his chin, as if to point out exactly where he'd like to receive his scratches, and Zya obliged. She loved him more than anything else. Well, *almost* anything else. Anyone but Elijah. Zya and Elijah had known each other since they were five or six, and the two were basically inseparable. He was a grade ahead and balanced Zya's impulsive, headstrong nature, with a more cautious and soft-spoken approach. Eli was always tinkering, and anything with gears and circuits was fair game.

"You should be an inventor, or something," she'd said the last time they were together, as she watched him work on a circuit board.

"That'd be cool," he said, shrugging his shoulders, attention glued to his latest obsession.

He was quiet and, yet, Zya got the feeling he wanted more than he let on. In that way, they were the same. She had such little control over her life. And, on top of that, for some reason, adults always assumed she was incapable of making decisions or thinking for herself. It was infuriating. All she wanted was respect, and she didn't think she was asking for too much. Just wait, they'd say. Appreciate your childhood. But none of them seemed to understand.

Zya was a dreamer. All around her, strewn across the bed, lay pads and pieces of paper with notes, drawings, story snippets and songs. Zya's mother was protective and, so, often, she was forced to imagine the world rather than experience it for herself. So, imagine she did. Zya dreamed of heroes and heroines, dragons and pirates, and precocious children traversing the galaxy. But not her. No, to Zya, sometimes it didn't feel like she was going anywhere, like life was just passing her by. Sunrises and sunsets, family dinners, and trips to school and back. It all slipped by with the kind of speed you could only understand when you're perfectly unmoved. More than anything else, she just wanted to be free. To feel real, make her own decisions and control her life. When she was big enough, Zya decided, she'd go anywhere she wanted, whenever she wanted to. But, it wasn't up to her right now, and it sucked. Big time.

Zya loved her mom. A lot. But there were just some things she couldn't talk about with her. She'd always been able to relate more on that level with her father. He always listened, at least. But it'd been years since they'd moved away and, to tell you the truth, she didn't really know him anymore. Sure, they'd seen each other once or twice when he came to town on business. But that just wasn't enough, and most of the warm memories of youth were long gone by now. She remembered feeling good when they were together but, anymore, she almost couldn't remember the feeling at all. Sometimes, she wondered why he didn't want to see her. Zya dreamed up reasons that would make it better. An explanation that would make her heart hurt less. Maybe he'd become a criminal mastermind, orchestrating global crimes like a James Bond villain. Or, maybe, he was a paragon of virtue, a literal modern-day saint, working to feed and clothe the poor. But, no matter what she imagined she couldn't shake the feeling that she wanted him here.

She tried to cry but her body almost wouldn't let her. She didn't want to do *that* anymore. The tears were too much, and she didn't like feeling out of control. But, all of a sudden, memories — of him pushing her on the swings, washing dishes together, and riding bikes — flashed through her mind. And, as she smiled a nostalgic smile, a single tear slid gracefully down her cheek.

"Zya!" her mother yelled up the stairs. "Dinner's ready."

"Coming." Zya yelled back.

She lingered at the window for just another moment. Zya didn't want to go downstairs. Not now. Not like this. The only true peace she had to herself was here. Well, here and in the forest, where she could climb trees and run as fast as she wanted. But she knew if she didn't go now her mother would be back, and she wouldn't be happy about it. So, she wiped her eyes with the sleeve of her shirt and, giving Herc a healthy pat, reluctantly gathered herself.

Zya was tall and lanky with butterscotch skin. Her small, round nose and sharp eyebrows were striking for a child of twelve. Full cheeks led down to a button chin that balanced the rest of her face. She wore a pair of Levi's jeans, black t-shirt with the word "fearless" written on the front in gold glitter, and topped off the getup with a pair of mismatched socks. Bounding down the stairs like a wild banshee, she slid into the kitchen and popped perfectly into her chair, not a moment too late. Zya's mother stood in front of the stove, and the sizzle of freshly breaded drumsticks dancing in hot oil played on her eardrums like a symphony.

"Mmmm, my favorite," she said, licking her lips.

"I thought you'd like that," said her mother, without turning.

And, even though she couldn't see her face, Zya could tell her mother was smiling. Her mom placed a drumstick and a thigh on a plate next to mac and cheese, mashed potatoes and broccoli, and placed the plate in front of her. Antonio, her mom's live-in boyfriend, was already digging in, so Zya sunk her teeth into the crunchy skin. She took another bite, and wondered, while chewing, why her mom and

Antonio didn't just get married already. But that was adult stuff, she told herself, shrugging off the thought.

"I'm tellin' ya," he said, in-between crunches. "You could sell this stuff."

Zya rolled her eyes. Her mom's cooking was good, but it wasn't first-place-at-the-State-Fair-good.

"Good?" her mother asked over her shoulder.

"Mmhmmm," Zya said, mouth packed to the brim.

Zya didn't like to brag, but she was a bit of a genius. Socially, that is. She knew how to say just enough to satisfy the grown-ups without saying too much. That was the trick: don't say too much. She almost always got in trouble when she said too much. It was a delicate balance and she played the game well. Then, again, as an only child, she'd been dealing with them her whole life.

"I was planning to meet up with Elijah after dinner," Zya said, swallowing her food.

"It's the first day of school tomorrow," her mother said, without looking up. "You need to get your rest."

Zya took another bite. She stared down at the table, avoiding eye contact.

But her mother didn't even turn around to witness the performance. "Besides, have you practiced your guitar today? You're not going anywhere until that's done. Don't forget you've got your voice lessons tomorrow night, too."

Zya let out a groan.

Her mother had had enough. Turning around, she shot a look of daggers. "You can put that attitude right back where it came from, young lady."

This time, she waited for her mother to turn back to the stove before making a face. And, oh, it was a magnificent face, tongue thrust through her lips like a defiant little flagpole.

But Antonio caught her in the act. "Don't disrespect your mother like that," he said. "After all she does for you."

She made a face at him too. "You're not my father."

"No, he sure isn't," her mother snapped. "Antonio didn't walk out on us."

Zya dropped the unfinished drumstick on her plate and her chair screeched against the kitchen floor as she pushed herself back from the table.

"Don't test me," her mother warned.

Zya glared intently, like she was trying to make her mother disappear. And, then, in the lightest turn, she spoke with a calm, conciliatory tone. "I'd like to go to bed early, please."

"If you think that's best," her mother said, turning back to the food.

Zya was furious. All of her pent up frustration was on the verge of boiling over. She fantasized about stomping her way up the stairs, but she knew that was a shortcut to a whoopin', so she restrained herself. She walked straight up to the second floor, through her bedroom door and locked it behind her with a "click". She was tempted to pout and feel sorry for herself, but she wasn't a baby anymore. She was twelve. Pouting was for babies. Besides, Zya knew throwing a tantrum wouldn't get her anywhere. So, she gathered herself with a big, deep breath, and a wave of calm washed over her. If she wanted something different, she'd have to do something different. And she knew what she had to do.

CHAPTER TWO

What Follows Is of Our Own Choosing

Zya plopped herself down on the side of her bed, grabbed her phone and sent Eli a text. *Meet u by the tree in 15?* She laced up her trusty pair of bright red Converse All-Stars, pulled a light black beanie over her shoulder-length braids and finished off the look with her favorite forest green bomber jacket. Zya hoisted her bedroom window and climbed out onto the slanted roof, shimmy-ing down the trellis on the side of the house. Just as her rubber soles hit the padded lawn, the phone buzzed in her pocket. It was Elijah. *Not if I beat you there.* Zya smiled, taking off at full speed.

"The tree" was a full-figured, two hundred year-old oak, hidden back in the not-so-little forest between their subdivisions. They hadn't quite turned it into a treehouse — it deserved to stay wild with the other trees — but they'd installed a tire swing and nailed a handful of two-by-fours into the trunk for a foothold. In this way, they were able to climb all the way to the top. Zy and Eli had come here so many times over the years. It felt like their own little Terabithia, a magical place where anything could happen and imagination was alive. Zya felt like herself when she propped up in its branches. They'd sit there for hours talking about their lives, parents, why ants always seem to walk single file or, quite possibly, absolutely nothing at all.

"Do you think we'll be like the adults when we grow up?" Zya asked Elijah one sunny afternoon, as they sat there, high in the branches of the Old Oak.

"I don't know," Elijah said. "I guess. Why?"

"Sometimes I don't wanna," she said. "I don't get them."

Elijah nodded. "Like when they want you to do something and you ask why, and all they say is 'Because I told you so'?"

She sighed. "Exactly."

"It's almost like they can't remember what it was like to be a kid," Elijah theorized.

Zya's eyes got big. "Do you think we're gonna forget what it's like to be ... *us*?"

"Honestly, I don't know," Elijah said in that rather matter-of-fact tone he'd take every now and then.

"I wonder what happened to them," Zya said.

"Well," Elijah un-wedged his foot to start back down. "Maybe we'll turn out different."

Zya was a strong runner. In fact, Elijah had started prodding her to try out for track and field. He was silly, that's what he was. Besides, high school wasn't for another couple years, and the middle school tryouts weren't till spring. So, she didn't have to decide anything just yet. At that very moment, she popped through the trees and spotted her friend, standing underneath the Old Oak, panting, hands on his hips.

"Took you long enough," Elijah said with a mischievous side-eyed smirk, as they greeted each other with their very own secret handshake.

"Honestly, it's a miracle I'm even here."

"There's something I need to show you," he said, without any pomp or circumstance. "Follow me."

They went urgently, and yet, at a comfortable pace. As Zy and Eli ran, the leaves and branches crackled underfoot. There was a kind of peace, and rhythm, to their stride. It was the kind of jog-run only a teenager can execute properly, almost clumsy and, yet, efficient in its own right. The sun was just starting to set and, soon enough the light would be gone. Even now, it began to wane, so that Zya had to strain her eyes.

"How much farther?" she asked.

"It's just over here," Elijah said, speeding up the hill.

Zya followed and, indeed, as they reached the top, she could see a blue-ish, white glow oozing through the trees ahead. By the time she caught up, Eli was bent over, hands on his knees, and, for some reason, she could only see his outline. Zya caught her breath. Now, she could see why. Behind her friend was the source of the soft blue light. It appeared, at first glance, to be shaped like a door. But this door didn't have any hinges, or a handle, and it didn't have a frame either. In fact, there was nothing else, whatsoever. Even more astounding was that they were able to walk around it, as if it led to nothing at all, and was merely a paper-thin hallucination. But they were looking at it, just the same.

"Amazing, huh?" Elijah said, less like a question and more like a compliment.

"How?" Zya asked, staring at it in awe.

"I found it last night while I was out here. I could feel something ... tugging at me, and it led me here."

"So, what do you think it is?" she asked.

"Seems to be a gateway — a portal — of some sort."

"What makes you think that?"

"Well, for one, it checks off all the boxes: glowing, gives off supernatural vibes ... and, oh yeah," he said. "It looks like a door."

Zya smiled. "Where do you think it goes?"

"No idea," he answered. "But I'd love to know how it works."

"Well," she said, "Let's find out."

"Find out?"

"I mean, it's a portal, right?" she asked. "Portals are meant to go through."

"I don't know, Zy," Elijah said.

"Oh, come on," she replied. "Aren't you even a little curious?"

"Of course I'm curious," he said. "But ..."

"But what?"

"Well," he started, "Who knows what's on the other side."

"Isn't that the point?" she asked.

Elijah got quiet. "I don't know if this is random, Zya. It's certainly not 'naturally occurring', which means ..."

"Someone placed it here on purpose."

"Bingo," he said. "I went home last night and combed Google ... there's never been anything like it documented ... *ever*."

They looked at each other and a streak of terror flashed across their eyes. But no feeling ever lasted too long, between friends, and their momentary fear quickly dissipated into curiosity. Who created it? What do they want? Why would they put it *here*?

"What if they're trying to get our attention?" Zya said.

Elijah cupped his chin with his hand, as if in thought. "But, why would an extra-terrestrial life form looking to make contact with human beings put a portal in the middle of a forest?"

Zya looked hard at Elijah. "Maybe they're trying to get *our* attention."

"Mmm," he said. "That would make sense. If they've observed us before they'd know that putting it here would make it likely we, and no one else, would find it. But, the question remains: *why?*"

Zya's eyes lit up. This is exactly what she'd been waiting for. A chance to take a leap, to do something different for a change.

"Well, then," she said. "What're we waiting for?"

Eli tilted his head to the left, scrunching up his nose and raising an eyebrow, in a look that said: *Elijah is currently unavailable. Please try again.*

"Come onnn," Zya said.

He exhaled. "It could be dangerous."

"Danger's my middle name," Zya said with a mischievous grin.

"It's not safe, Zy."

"Safe?" she rolled her eyes. "You sound like my mother."

"Oh, come on," Eli smiled. "You know what I meant. There's no way to know what's on the other side, and it might be something that wants to hurt us."

"You're right," Zya nodded. "Only one way to find out."

And, without another thought, she broke into a sprint.

"Zy!" Elijah tried to grab her wrist but it was too late.

Another half second and his friend slipped through the glowing door. Elijah shook his head. She was always like this. Headstrong and stubborn. Ironically, it was one of the things he loved about her. So, Elijah was faced with a choice: stay put and make his friend face uncertainty alone, or follow her through and take on the challenge together. *I'd really rather not*, he said to himself, *but you have to*. There was no way he was going to let his friend down. He let out a heavy sigh and, then, with a flash, the forest was silent.

CHAPTER THREE

To Be, Or Not To Be

Indeed, the glowing door *was* a portal, just as they'd suspected. And so quick it was, that, like the blinking of an eye, the children passed from one world to another. It was like stepping out of your bedroom and into the great unknown. It was a leap of faith. A leap that started in Zy and Eli's little forest and ended as their shoes hit a smooth, hard floor.

Elijah stumbled, but regained his balance without falling. He looked ahead and could see Zya gazing out a floor-to-ceiling window. On the other side was a stunningly spectacular view of outer space. Yes, the kind with stars, planets and a big, black void. That far-off place they'd learned about in school, that captures the imagination of science fiction authors and TV writers, and seems so far away you could only dream about it. You know the stories about space travel, advanced alien societies and geologically improbable planets that are made up of one, *single* ecosystem.

"Woah," he said, awestruck. "Is that ... real?"

Zya nodded. "Sure looks real."

Thousands of stars, scattered throughout the darkness, shining their little faces off. And, smack-dab in the middle, a green and blue planet that looked a lot like Earth. Zya thought she could make out the continent of Africa floating amongst the blue ocean. She reached out her hand, gently placing her palm on the window. The ship was warm to the touch, and pulsated with energy, as if it might have been alive.

"Feels real, too," she said.

The corridor they were in was about ten feet tall and twenty-five or thirty feet wide, every surface smooth to the touch. The silver walls sparkled like a showerhead after a good shine and gave the space a feeling of sterility. The hallway curved to the right and the two younguns cautiously followed the bend. But, before they were able to take more than a handful of steps, they spotted a strange figure coming toward them. The creature was tall and skinny, with a long, purple robe covering its lanky frame. It had huge black eyes, blue-grey skin and an unusually long neck.

"Hello, and welcome to the Nimrod." The creature spoke musically, even though it didn't seem to open its mouth. *Did it even have a mouth?*

Elijah chimed in. "What's a 'Nimrod'?"

The creature laughed. "The Nimrod is the flagship of the Lumerian Intergalactic Fleet."

Zya raised an eyebrow. "And who are you?"

"I am Kelven," they said with a soft smile. "And, I will be your guide while you are on board."

Kelven's face was very much like what most people might think an alien would look like. Big eyes, long nostrils, skin like a seal and absolutely zero sign of hair. Kelven didn't seem to have an easily definable gender, either. They spoke with a voice one might call a man's, but something as consequential as their facial features were undoubtedly feminine. They were tall, perhaps as tall as seven feet, and walked regally, holding their oblong head high. Though they'd only just met, there was something in the Lumerian's soft voice that felt comforting, and it put the friends at ease.

"You must have so many questions," they said. "But, first, please, follow me to the bridge. Maroun is waiting for you."

"How can we hear you?" Zya asked, as they walked.

"We do not speak with words, but with our minds," Kelven responded.

"Does that mean you can read our minds?" Elijah inquired.

"No," Kelven responded. "It's different than thinking. It's more like directing a thought. Thoughts that are yours remain yours."

Just then, a pressurized door slid open and they were standing on the bridge. It was a spectacular sight. The walls were gilded with shiny metal and ornamental glass, giving the ship an air of sophistication. It was too pretty to be a warship — diplomatic, perhaps — but it was clear they were technologically advanced. There was a large viewscreen at the front, along with a pair of navigation stations, spaced equal distance apart, at which two lanky aliens sat, tip-tapping away.

"What's this thing made of?" Elijah asked, running his hand over the bulkhead.

"The hull is made from a solid Tritanium alloy," Kelven responded.

"Tritanium?" Elijah asked with a confused look.

"It's not found on your world," Kelven said, "but it's about twenty times harder than a diamond."

"Twenty times?" Elijah exclaimed.

"The rest is made up of gold, silver, pressure-proof glass and an aluminum-graphite alloy."

"Hmmm." Elijah stroked his chin and wrinkled his brow, as if peering into some far-off dimension.

Just then, the captain's chair in the center of the bridge swung around and in it sat another alien. This one, whose dark brown robes perfectly complemented its rust-colored skin, was particularly keen-looking. The deeper skin tone stood out among the Lumerians and was honored for its uniqueness. The creature, who Zya and Elijah presumed was the ship's captain, rose from his seat. And, as he did, they could see he wasn't quite as androgynous as Kelven, either. As he came toward them, they could see, even despite the long, flowing robes, that he was notably more muscular. But he also moved in a friendly manner.

"Thank you for escorting our guests safely, Kelven," he said, turning to them. "I am Maroun."

"Zya," she said. "And this is Elijah."

"Zya," he nodded, "Elijah. We've been expecting you."

"So, the door *was* for us!" Elijah exclaimed.

"Yes, my child."

"Why?" Zya butted in. "Why us?"

"Because you are the only ones who can save humanity."

"*Us?*" Elijah blurted out, shocked.

So far, everything had been a little unbelievable — the door, the ship, the fact that, either, they were in a dream or face-to-face with aliens — but this seemed particularly far-fetched. He must have them confused with someone else.

"You must have it wrong," Zya said. "We're just kids."

"We *know* who you are," Maroun said calmly, "And this is why it must be you."

The alien captain walked between the two pilot stations, closer to the main viewscreen. And, without so much as a command, the display zoomed in close on the planet below. Now, just as before, Zya could clearly see Africa. It looked a little bigger, and a slightly different shape than she remembered, but it was undeniable now.

"This is Earth," Maroun said.

"Is that right?" Zya said snarkily.

He gave her a look and continued. "It's the year nine thousand seven hundred twenty-one and the Archons, a power-hungry race of lizard aliens, have ruled the planet for a thousand years."

"Wait," said Elijah. "Did you say ... *nine thousand*?"

"Yes."

"As in ... seventy-seven hundred years in the future?"

"Actually," Maroun said, "We're in the past."

"The past?!" both children said at once.

"So, let me get this straight," Elijah asked rather uncomfortably. "You're saying evil aliens with advanced technology enslaved humanity almost twelve thousand years ago?"

"Precisely," said Maroun. "Although ..."

"Although, what?" Zya asked.

"Well," he clarified, "Since we're actually *here*, it's technically happening right now."

"So, time travel *is* possible," Elijah said, astonished.

"Time is always happening," Maroun said calmly. "Some species, including ours, have evolved the ability to grasp and experience the simultaneity of it all."

Zya's brow was furrowed and it looked like her mind was working on overdrive.

"I understand if this is jarring for you," he went on. "So, take your time."

After a long moment, Zya said, "You still haven't answered my question. Why does it have to be us?"

"The two of you hold the key to victory," Maroun said, gesturing to the pair. "*You* are humanity's final hope."

CHAPTER FOUR

You, and Only You, Can Save Us

Zya took a moment to gather herself. There she was, on the bridge of an alien ship, looking down at her homeworld from space. It hadn't felt, even an hour ago, as she sat alone in her room, that this was a remote possibility. Even though she'd asked for this very thing, she was stunned by the turn of events. On top of everything, a seven-foot alien who communicates via telepathy was trying to tell her that she and her lanky nerd-of-a-friend were humanity's only hope to stop a race of evil aliens from enslaving Earth forever.

"But, we're not slaves where we come from," Elijah pointed out. "Maybe it works itself out."

"Well, actually," Maroun explained, "By the time the two of you are born, any Archons who managed to remain on Earth have figured out that the way to wield power best is to do it from the shadows."

"That way," Zya interjected, "Everybody *thinks* they're free, but they're not."

"Precisely."

"Okay, you're gonna have to start from the beginning," Zya said. "Tell us everything."

Maroun smiled. "The Archons are born of the same galaxy as our race. In fact, we were only a solar system away."

Images flashed across the viewscreen. "We identified their penchant for conquest early on, but weren't in any position to stop them. While the Archons craved conflict, we focused internally. They quickly spread through their solar system and, before long, developed the technology to travel outside it.

"By the time we developed faster-than-light travel, they'd already populated multiple planets. Because of our contemplative ways, we were late bloomers. In a way, it set us back, but it also kept us from being reckless. Eventually, we, too, found our way into space. But, instead of focusing on colonization, we pioneered breakthroughs in sustainable energy, social cohesion, and societal efficiency. And, only a few hundred years after discovering faster-than-light, we developed the blink drive, granting our ships the ability to travel seamlessly through space and time, itself.

"By then, the Archons had ventured out even farther, enslaving dozens of worlds, and leaving governors to rule each one. See, while we were solving our energy crisis, the Archons never did. They only consume and, therefore, must constantly find ways to replenish their resources. Their hunger has enslaved them, and it always asks for more."

"So, why don't *you* stop them?" Zya asked sharply. "What with your time-traveling space ships and all."

"Yeah," Elijah agreed. "What could we do that you can't?"

"We can't interfere directly." Maroun shook his head. "The Archons are powerful. In a head-to-head contest, we'd likely be overwhelmed. We're only one planet and they have an empire behind them. The only way we've been able to survive this long is by hiding."

"With what?" Elijah scoffed. "A cloaking device?"

"Essentially, yes," Maroun responded, as the boy's eyes grew even bigger. "It was one of our first mass-mobilizations after we entered space."

"Can I see it?"

Zya elbowed Eli in the side, as if to say, *shut up.*

Maroun smiled, as if amused. "When this is done, we'll show you anything you like. But, right now, time is of the essence."

"But you still haven't told us why we're here," Zya said.

"*We* can't interfere," Maroun repeated. "But *you're* human."

"I get it," Zya turned up her nose. "You want us to do your dirty work."

"It's true," Maroun started. "Though we're not directly at fault, we do feel a certain ... responsibility. Some back home on Lumen believe that had we been more willing to engage the Archons directly it might have helped them learn a healthy lesson. We might have grown together, side-by-side. Instead, we chose seclusion, and they set out to conquer the universe. So, we're just trying to do our part, but we can't do it all for you."

"This still doesn't make sense," Zya asked. "Why *us*?"

The Lumerian turned and gave her his full attention. It was a little uncomfortable, at first, if Zya was being honest. But Maroun was a powerful being, and she felt honored by his gaze.

"You are special," he said. "Guardians are carefully hand-selected, as were the two of you. You may not understand who you are just yet, but I do, and I need you to trust me. This is what you were made for, and your people need you now."

For a moment, there was silence. "Okay," Zya said. "We'll help."

"We will?" Elijah asked, his face all scrunched up.

She turned and met his eyes. "I need you Eli. Don't make me do this alone."

Elijah pursed his lips and looked into the corner of the room, as if searching for a lightbulb, or another portal out of here. But, of course he wasn't going to let her do this by herself. If that was the plan, he would've stayed back in the forest.

"You know I can't let you have *all* the fun" he smirked, turning to Maroun. "As long as you promise to show me that cloaking device."

So, it was decided. They followed Maroun off the bridge, down another hallway into a mid-sized room that, at first glance, appeared nearly empty. Upon further investigation, Zya spotted a dozen or so sleek laser pistols on the wall behind them. Opposite the wall, on the hull side, was a large bay window, with yet another view of space. But they weren't here for the laser guns, or the sightseeing. In the very center of the room sat a lone display case, which Maroun sauntered over to, the children closely in tow. There, inside the case, were two small, half-open black boxes. Inside each, a shiny timepiece glistened in the light. The watches were made of the purest gold, and trimmed with the finest silver. Each device had three hands, indecipherable inscriptions around the dial and an open face, so that one could see all the wheels, gears and drivers that made it go 'round.

Maroun casually deactivated the containment field and plucked the boxes from inside, presenting one to each of them.

"These are for you," he said.

"What? Woah!" Elijah couldn't hold back his excitement, as he examined the item from every direction.

Zya took hers out of the box and strapped it on her wrist. "What does it do?"

"Look at any place in this room," Maroun directed. "Look at any place in the room and wish you were there."

Elijah closed his eyes and wrinkled his nose, but nothing happened.

"You're doing it *all* wrong," Zya teased, rolling her eyes with a playful smile. The next moment, she was gone. Elijah whipped his head around, scouring the corners for any sign of his friend. But, before he had a chance to worry, she reappeared on the far side of the room, right by the big bay window.

Elijah blinked in surprise.

"Like Maroun said," Zya coached. "Just look at a spot and imagine yourself there."

Elijah focused on the opposite corner, envisioning himself standing there, gazing back into his own eyes. As he conjured the image in his mind, the drivers of the watch turned a bright, glowing gold, spinning, and spinning, and causing the gears to go faster, and faster, and faster. The third hand was going so fast it looked like a thin layer of gold film, stretched over the face of the watch. And, as it continued to spin, round, and round, and round, that film spread over Elijah's skin, until he was fully enveloped. Then, in the snap of a finger, he was gone, and everything was still.

"Sweet!"

The voice sounded like Elijah but it came from the other corner of the room. It had all happened so fast. There he was, back to the wall, in the opposite corner, staring at the very spot he'd been only moments before.

"The powers of the timepiece aren't limitless," Maroun warned. "You can only go as far as you can see."

"Anything else we should know?" Zya asked, raising an eyebrow.

"As long as they are strapped to your wrist, there is no limit to how many times you can jump, but they do take a couple seconds to cool off."

"Okay. So ..." Elijah looked at the ceiling, as if making a calculation. He jumped, reappearing a split-second later in almost the exact same spot. Once he'd replicated the experiment a satisfactory amount of times, he turned to Zya and Maroun.

"Two-and-a-half seconds," he said. "We've got two-and-a-half seconds."

"That's not long," Zya remarked.

"To some," Maroun said quietly, "It's an eternity."

CHAPTER FIVE

If You Didn't Know, Now You Know

The newly minted intergalactic heroes jumped back and forth across the room, from one side to another. As they familiarized themselves with the watches, Maroun looked on with a satisfied smile. Eventually, the orientation was over and Zya turned to the tall, rust-colored Lumerian.

"What would happen if I put myself out there?" she said, gesturing to the cold, dark void beyond the bay window.

"Well," Elijah interjected, "There's absolutely *zero* oxygen. But that's the least of your worries. First, your blood is going to boil, and then it's gonna freeze, and there's a good chance your heart explodes before your eyes pop out of your head ..."

"Elijah..." Zya said quietly.

"I'm just saying," he went on. "If you don't get the jump right the first time ..."

"Indeed," Maroun jumped in. "The boy is right. Your confidence is your greatest strength but ... if you go too far, too quickly, there's a chance you might never come back."

Eli smiled ear to ear and puffed out his chest.

"However," Maroun added. "It is also true that one can only find the wrinkles in time while pushing the boundaries of what's possible.

So, choose your spots wisely, my child. And, once you make up your mind, don't hesitate."

She wasn't used to people speaking to her like Maroun did, but she could feel that it was good for her. She was so used to adults issuing orders and talking down to her. This had a distinctly different feeling. She felt stronger, as if simply having his confidence meant something. She couldn't quite put her finger on *why*, but it felt real, nonetheless. It was like a subtle wave that began at the crown of her head and rippled down through her fingers and toes, as if she'd connected to some cosmic power source. Like she'd, simultaneously, been gifted a suit of armor and wrapped in the warmest blanket.

Zya examined the odd couple before her — the tall, skinny nerd and the elegant alien diplomat. One might have looked at them and deduced that they had little in common on the surface but she could feel that they were both on her side, and that was priceless. Zya could protect herself but, all the same, it was encouraging to know that she wouldn't be in this alone. It was comforting to know that there were those willing to go to the ends of the Earth with her.

"Thank you," she said. "Appreciate you."

"At your disposal, my child," Maroun said, bowing his head.

"Any time," Elijah said, with a wink, and they shook on it.

Nodding in approval, Maroun said, "Now, follow me."

He led them down another long hall. "One of the reasons the Archons have been so successful at oppressing the people of Earth is that they have found a way to harness the power of the The Pyramids."

"Pyramids? Like, the Great Pyramids of Giza?" Elijah interrupted. "In Egypt?"

"It's called Kemet, here. But, yes," Maroun explained patiently. "We've detected a low frequency vibrational energy wave spread over most of the known world, and it's originating from the Great Pyramid Complex. Somehow, it seems, they've been able to utilize the Nile's water to create the energy wave and project it into the atmosphere.

From there, the current is conducted by strategically placed obelisks and pyramids across the region."

"But, why," Elijah asked.

"We're not sure, exactly," Maroun answered. "But it's likely to elicit some kind of biological response."

Zya gasped. "They're trapped."

"Quite perceptive, daughter." Maroun explained. "This is our concern, as well. We fear the Archons have utilized their superior technology to suppress the will of the people. For a Lumerian, this is the greatest crime of all, to take a people's sovereign right."

"And you need us because we haven't been suppressed," she concluded.

"Precisely."

"So, we have to disable The Pyramids, huh?"

"Yes, in a sense," Maroun said. "But it's not going to be that easy."

"Who said that sounded easy," Elijah muttered under his breath.

"Oh?" Zya asked. "Why's that?"

"Enki," said Maroun.

Zya raised an eyebrow.

"Enki is the local governor and fashions himself 'The Lord of Earth'. He rules from the Dynastic Throne in Memphis, while also acting as high priest. Enki is very powerful, hopelessly vain and extremely dangerous. He maintains his stranglehold on the population by employing a large network of spies and inflicting fear through public displays of violence."

"So, how are *we* supposed to beat him?" Elijah asked.

"The Emerald Tablets," Maroun said.

"What's that?" Elijah's eyes got big.

"An ancient artifact of untold power," Maroun responded. "They are said to have been created by the Archon Thoth, and operate on the principle of 'That which is below is like that which is above, and that which is above is like that which is below.'"

"How will that help us defeat this ... Enki?" Zya asked.

"It's a principle that can be twisted," Maroun answered. "But, in the hands of a pure and honest soul, can be used to great effect."

"What, exactly, do they do?" Zya pried.

"That secret is for you, and you alone," he said. "But, be warned. We've come into contact with one of these artifacts before, and it nearly destroyed us."

"There's more than one?" Elijah asked.

"There are seven," Maroun said. "Seven cosmic talismans, each of which holds a great secret."

"Where did they come from?"

"Honestly? We're not sure," Maroun replied. "From all accounts, they predate even our own civilization. All we know for sure is that, somehow, for some reason, they've been scattered throughout space and time, like breadcrumbs. We suspect they are the key to defeating the Archons."

"Okay, so, how're we supposed to find these 'Emerald Tablets'?" Zya asked.

"We have good information that they are on Earth, somewhere in Memphis."

"What if the Archons already found them?" Zya asked.

"If they had, we would know by now," he said. "These tablets are of such immense power, they would pose a great danger in the hands of the Archons. This is why you must find them first. Now, we haven't been able to pinpoint the tablets, which is unusual, considering that they are said to be a source of immense power."

"What if they're being disguised somehow?" Elijah asked, as they passed through another pressure-sealed door.

"Perceptive, young man," Maroun said. "A great deal of energy is naturally emitted from the pyramid complex, which could act as a shield for the tablets. It seems as good a place as any to start."

"Wait," Zya interjected. "If the Archons haven't been able to uncover the tablets in ... uh, a *thousand* years, how, exactly, do you think we're gonna be able to just waltz down there and find them?"

"Because," he responded. "You are on the side of good, and the Universe is pulling for you."

"Oh," Zya said, unimpressed. "Well, *that* makes me feel better."

"Oh, young one," Maroun said calmly. "I've been here long enough to know that, sometimes, all that makes the difference is timing, and we have it on good information that the timing is perfect — that is why we are here, and why we called for you. It is your arrival, which has been foretold, that will cause the wheels of change to turn."

Then, Maroun walked up to the extra-large display console, bravely standing in the middle of the room alone, and invited the children to the other side of the room, where they were greeted by a raised platform with four glowing circles.

"A *transporter*?" Elijah asked in disbelief.

"Ah, yes," said the Lumerian, with a bit of a laugh. "Star Trek, right?"

From the folds of his robe, the Lumerian diplomat produced two small metallic disks, which sprung to life in his palm. Four tiny legs shot out of each side and Zya couldn't help but recoil. They reminded her of two tiny robot spiders. She *hated* spiders. And, Zya was convinced robot spiders were even creepier. Elijah, on the other hand, was curious and took a step closer, to get a better look.

He cocked his head to one side. "What are they?"

"Universal translators," Maroun said. "You can understand us because we speak to you in your own language, but you'll need these to understand anyone outside the Nimrod."

"How do they work?" Elijah asked.

"They interface directly with your eardrum, instantly translating any language in real time," Maroun explained. "So, you'll hear what they're saying, as they're saying it."

"When you say 'interface directly,'" Zya asked, hesitantly, "you don't mean ..."

"They must crawl through your ear canal," Maroun said casually. "Hence the streamlined design."

But, Zy didn't hear anything after, "crawl through your ear canal."

"Nope," she said. "No way."

Elijah went over to his friend. "Come on, Zy. I know you don't like the creepy crawlies. But just ... imagine it's—"

"Nuh uh," she said, closing her eyes. "I can't."

"Please, don't say that," he implored. "I need you. We all need you, right now."

"Ugh," Zya sighed, cocking her head to the side. "You know, sometimes I really hate you."

"No, you don't," Elijah said.

"You're right, I don't hate you," she said. "But sometimes I really want to."

"Please lean your head to the side," Maroun said. "You'll only feel a slight tickle."

Zya closed her eyes in preparation, tensing her muscles tightly and shrugging her shoulders as high as they could go. After a few seconds, she peeked an eye open.

"Watcha waitin' for?"

Maroun gave a hearty laugh. "It's already done, my child."

Already done? She hadn't felt a thing. Zya quickly concluded the whole ordeal wasn't half as bad as she'd made it up to be. But she was glad it was over, all the same. The children walked toward the platform as Maroun went to work, his long arms and fingers punching in coordinates with purpose.

"I'm thinking it would be best to put you down by the smallest pyramid," Maroun glanced up. "What do you think?"

Elijah shook his head. "I'm just trying to figure out ..."

"Yes?" Maroun inquired, as his hands continued to work.

"Well," Elijah said, as he stepped on the glowing circle. "Our scientists don't think the pyramids were built until the year four thousand."

"I don't remember hearing anything about lizard aliens in history class either," Zya quipped.

Maroun smiled, as he made the final calculations. "It's just proof that you can never know the truth until you see it for yourself."

The Guardians locked eyes. Elijah had a million questions written all over his face, but Zya could see that he wouldn't be swayed. Not now. She was afraid, too, but they refused to let it show. There was something that needed to be done, and they needed to do it. She winked at Elijah, and he gave her a glint of mischievous curiosity. *It was on.*

The Lumerian captain looked up and his face was filled with solemn concern. "Your people need you," he said "They're counting on you."

In unison, the Guardians nodded at Maroun.

"Don't forget," he said. "No matter what happens, you always have each other."

Zya stole one last look at her friend, and wondered what lay ahead for them.

"We'll be monitoring the planet," Maroun said. "So, just give us a call if you need anything."

"Well, isn't that comforting," Elijah said.

"One more thing."

"Yes?" Zya answered.

"Please," he said. "Come back in one piece."

CHAPTER SIX

What's the Difference Between Trouble and Adventure?

Zya blinked and, all of a sudden, the ship's pristine interior was gone. In its place, a vast desert materialized. The sun was low in the sky and there was nothing but sand in all directions. She looked up and felt small in the shadow of the "smallest" Great Pyramid. It was indescribably massive in scope, overshadowing the encampment they now found themselves standing in. All three of the giant, graduated monuments were lined up in ascending order, one behind the other, so they almost looked like a set of Matryoshka dolls. They stood still, transfixed by the majestic magnificence before them.

"Boy, this'll be some story," Eli said.

"Yeah," Zya said. "Too bad no one will believe it."

So they stopped and drank the moment in, lingering in that space between worlds, where there are no peasants and no kings, just awareness. Soaking up the seconds, they stored the memory deep in their hearts and minds. Never again would they have this moment. Never again would they experience it for the first time. You know, they say you only get one chance to make a first impression, and these wonders of the world really stuck the landing.

But, as the world always does, it came knocking. As if out of nowhere (although, that's ridiculous because everything comes from *somewhere*), a small desert mouse scampered into view, sniffing up a storm and scurrying all about. It was as if the little fella was searching for something, Zya thought, and absolutely determined to find it. Elijah watched the creature's long whiskers gently caress the sand as it flitted about from one tiny dune to the next. At each little sandy indentation, it would stop and sniff, meticulously checking every inch before moving on. So, Zya was surprised when, suddenly, the rodent thrust its nose in the air, sniffed furiously and then scampered out of sight.

"I wonder what that was all about," Eli said under his breath.

"Shhhh," Zya hissed.

They listened intently, straining their ears.

After a moment, Elijah spoke again. "What is it?"

"Be quiet," Zya spat out the words.

They listened again. All was still and quiet.

"This way," she said, walking briskly toward the pyramid.

The two gangly teens navigated their way through the shanty town. Without knowing how, Zya could feel her gut talking, and she felt uneasy. It was as if some tragedy had taken place where they were standing. *I bet the workers lived here*, Zya thought, wondering how long it had been in disrepair. The dwellings were pathetic and nothing was taller than seven or eight feet. The windows were either open or boarded up and, somehow, the doors were all hanging off their hinges, just like they were waiting to fall off. It was as if every room had been assembled out of leftover materials meant for something else.

"This place gives me the creeps," Elijah said.

Zya rolled her eyes. "Oh, relax," she said. "It's not like it's *haunted*."

But, just as the words escaped her mouth, two ghastly forms crawled around the edge of a nearby shack and floated — yes, *floated* — directly between them and the pyramid. The apparitions were dirty, mangled and dripping in tattered rags. They lingered there, eyeing the children and running their ghastly tongues over their ghastly teeth.

"What a catch," said the skinny one.

"Beauts," said the other, who, curiously enough, even as a ghost, was a bit portly.

Zya and Elijah locked eyes and, without a word, took off, back the way they'd come. Even though Elijah was older — and, hence, had longer legs — Zya was a speedster in her own right. Her calves were especially powerful and she used her natural twitch to get just a little more out of each stride. So, they ran, as fast as they possibly could. The two youths tore through the shanty town, sliding round corners, as they twisted and turned through the narrow streets. The menacing figures were hot on their tail. Zya glanced over her shoulder and noticed the skinny one skimming the rooftops. She could see the moon slicing through the apparition's translucent body, leaving nothing more than a smoky outline against the sky. Then, all of a sudden, it made a move and swooped at her.

"Jump!" Zya yelled.

She struck out and Elijah followed suit. In the heat of the moment, they'd nearly forgotten about the timepieces but now they were jumping and running, and running and jumping, over roofs, and through alleyways, with the Fiends fast on their heels. From above, they must've looked like little jitterbugs, jumping over the surface of a pond, with one child at a time jumping ahead, running as fast as they could and then jumping again. The Fiends were fast — it helps, of course, when you've got no bones, or conscience, to get in the way — but the young Guardians were faster. Anytime one of the ghouls was about to grab them, all it would take was a quick teleport to put them back out of reach. So, they played the same game, over and over again. Zya had never felt faster, and she could see Elijah was having fun too.

The sun was just about to disappear over the horizon, and the shadows stretched far as the eye could see. The perilous game of cat-and-mouse migrated across the desert like dance partners moving across the floor. They were in the open sand now, and the Great

Pyramid was getting bigger and bigger. As they got closer, the monument grew exponentially in size, opening up to devour the sky like a massive mouth.

The spirits hadn't laid a single, sinewy finger on them, but it seemed they just wouldn't give up. *They probably don't get tired*, Zya realized, wondering just how long they'd have to play this song-and-dance before they'd leave. Just then, a sleek, silver, bullet-shaped craft zipped out from behind the Great Pyramid and was on top of them in the twinkling of an eye. It was fast and powerful, and cut them off in a matter of seconds. Two bright spotlights, which emanated from its nose, were pointed in their direction and rotated in a figure-eight. Then, altogether, the headlights snapped forward and engulfed the Guardians in a blinding light. For a second, Zya felt like she was back on stage again. She put on the brakes, digging her heels into the desert floor, and Elijah stopped cold. As for the Fiends, whether allergic to the lights or simply not interested, they retreated, releasing a chorus of blood-curdling wails on their way back to the shantytown.

The friends stood shoulder to shoulder. The lights were so bright they couldn't see anything else. As the vehicle hovered closer, Zya raised her arm to shield her eyes, and felt Elijah grab her other hand. She squeezed him back and held on for dear life. Then, almost exactly as they left the Nimrod, their sandy surroundings started to fade, and the two friends re-materialized inside the mysterious flying object.

They looked around, in an attempt to gain their bearings, but it was too dark to see. The only sliver of light came from the cold white-ish-blue glow of a force field. Once their eyes adjusted to the light, it became apparent they were in some sort of cell. The walls were cold and hard, and they were trapped. *The irony*, Zya thought. *To come all this way and end up in a little room we can't leave.* They heard the sound of a hatch open, and Zya could sense another presence. It did not immediately make itself known but, as they waited patiently, out of the darkness and into the glow, came the flicking tongue of a life-sized serpent. Next, they caught sight of its head, which Zya thought looked like one of those Velociraptors from Jurassic Park. Only bigger, taller and with opposable thumbs.

"Looksss what we've gotsss hereee," the lizard taunted, as it flicked its tongue in and out.

Zya crossed her arms and rolled her eyes. "Oh, so, this is what we're doing? A villain monologue? You know those never work."

"You know," Eli looked back-and-forth from the talking lizard, to his brave friend. "She *is* right."

"Shhhhhhh, Prissonerssss!" The alien hissed, moving its neck back-and-forth in a menacing, S-like motion.

"Don't worry, we won't be here much longer," Zya said casually. "And, then, you'll have all the quiet you want."

This agitated the creature, causing it to hiss, and writhe uncontrollably. They could hear it muttering under its breath.

"The hum-maans thinksss wesss not ssssmarttt," said the Archon, as it held up one of its long, green fingers. Hanging there, like two loose rings, were their timepieces.

As if by reflex, the children felt for their wrists, but the bands were gone. *We're in deep trouble*, Zya thought.

"Ssssoon enoughhh," said the beast, "You will ssstand before Hiss Highnesss and he will deal with you himssselffff."

"'His Highness'?" Elijah said. "Oh, you mean Enki?"

The lizard hissed even louder, bringing his head right up to the force field, so that his snout was nearly touching it. The movement was so quick, the children both jumped back, despite the existence of the force field.

"No one speaksss hisss nameee," the lizard hissed. "The Lord of Earth, Pharaoh of the Dynassstic Throne, High Priessst to the Godsss, may he be honored."

Wow, Zya thought, *Maroun was serious about all that "Lord of Earth" stuff*. And it was then that she realized they were truly in a different world, a world that wasn't made for them. A world that was dangerous, because they represented change, and the world did not want to change. But there was no way back now. The only way was forward.

"Well," she said, with a tinge of sarcasm, "I hope the Lord of Earth will forgive me."

CHAPTER SEVEN

Welcome to the Jungle

Before they had a chance to get used to their surroundings, the Guardians were being escorted off the craft. They stepped through the tight doorway and onto a boarding ramp, with their captor close behind, hissing at them all the way. The reptilian, they could now see in the palace lights, was even bigger than they'd first thought. Its name, they would later find out, was Isimud, Enki's right hand. The Archon general stood almost seven feet tall, dwarfing the teenagers. He wore a long, white loincloth around his waist, a white, hooded shawl over his head and the gold pauldrons of a general across his shoulders.

The platform, on which they stood, was elevated above the ground, so that the tips of the palace garden trees just barely peeked over. It was an impressive sight. In all directions, as far as the eye could see, despite the surrounding desert, everything here was lush, and green, and bursting with color. Pterodactyl-sized birds, primates, big cats, frogs, lizards and snakes were all easy to find in this fake paradise. Isimud directed them down a long elevated bridge that led toward the palace itself. Its massive stone walls and extravagant architecture towered over the city streets and cast a shadow on the buildings below.

Zya heard a whirring and looked up just in time to glimpse another UFO. This one was flat and round, like a standard flying saucer. It was bigger than the one they'd just been in, by magnitudes. Zya elbowed Elijah, and pointed at it. But, by the time he looked, it was nowhere to be seen.

"What?" he whispered.

She shook her head.

"I've got a bad feeling about this," Elijah said quietly, as the towering palace walls got closer and closer.

"Just stay close," she whispered. "And keep your eyes open."

Isimud led them between a cavalcade of pillars and Zya remembered thinking how curious it was that, despite a clearly advanced grasp of technology, it was wooden torches that lit these halls. She felt a sudden pang of fear. But, then, she remembered what her Grandma Anita would tell her when she was afraid. *The only way they win* — Zya imagined the voice so vividly it felt like she was really there — *is if you give them what they want. They wanna to break you, little one. Don't let them.* Though they were just words, they were worth more to Zya in that moment than anything else, and she thanked her lucky stars.

The halls were dark, and clean, except for the soot stains where the flames licked at the stone. Zya tried not to strain her eyes but couldn't help peering at the stories painted on the wall in hieroglyphics. She thought some of them looked scary, especially in the dark red glow of the torches. Scenes of priests, with newborns in hand, about to make sacrifice, and myths of the epic power struggle between Archons.

Then, the palace hallway opened up, light pouring in, and she realized they were entering the Throne Room. It was long and rectangular with twelve fourteen-meter pillars lining the long central pool on both sides. The ceiling was vaulted, with large rectangular cutouts that let in the warm night air. A sky full of stars shone down through the opening, their light dancing over the water. Enki's two pet crocodiles lounged in the pool like a pair of lazy degenerates as a healthy smattering of frogs rested, blissfully untouched, on their luxurious lily pads.

A movement on the far side of the room caught Zya's attention. On the other side of the pool, a man arrogantly reclined on an ornate throne. Upon seeing Isimud and the children, he rose. He stood at full height and it was apparent that he was even taller than Isimud. Eight feet, maybe, if she had to guess.

"It's him," Zya whispered to Elijah.

"I'd hope so," he responded. "He's wearing the Horned Crown."

Zya wrinkled her nose.

"I've been reading," he said shyly.

The crown was made of pure gold, with a big, flat gold disk perfectly filling the space between two curved antlers, also made out of gold. Pure golden bracers adorned his bronze shins and muscular forearms and, on his chest, a golden breastplate, made in the mold of a bird's wings. But it was his eyes that drew Zya's attention. They were bright blue, like the color of the sky, and burned with a fire not easily satisfied. As she watched, Zya could've sworn those bright, blue irises changed to a deep, searing yellow. But only for a moment, when he blinked. And she wondered if she was seeing things.

"Ahhh, the children." Enki's deep voice rumbled through the chamber.

"Yesss, massster," said Isimud, immediately falling to a knee.

Then, without warning, the monarch began to vibrate. His cells were moving so fast, he didn't look solid at all. But, before another second had passed, it stopped, and there, before them, stood Enki. He was two full feet taller and nothing short of terrifying. Now, the yellow eyes were no longer an illusion but very, very real. They stared back at her, punctuated by the sinister-looking reptilian pupils. She knew it was probably unfair to judge, purely based on appearance, but she couldn't help thinking they simply looked evil. His teeth and claws were bigger too, almost one-and-a-half times those of Isimud. Perhaps it was just a ruler's disposition, but his tongue, though slithery in its own right, was more subdued than his general. Upon seeing his Lord reveal himself, Isimud bowed his head even lower.

Then, like a looking glass, Enki's gaze fell on the children. Zya could feel him, examining them, like cattle. There was not an inch of skin his eyes did not touch. In fact, the intensity of it nearly overwhelmed her, but she held onto her grandma's words. *There's too much at stake, Zya. Don't back down now.* She didn't like it, but there was nowhere to hide. So she resisted the urge to shrink and stood her ground. Next to her, she could see Elijah swaying, knock-kneed, as if overcome by some hypnotic trance. And, yet, somehow, he was still standing too.

Enki's presence was imposing. He commanded attention and loyalty, simply based on his stature. But there was something else lurking beneath the surface. This alien conqueror, who'd fashioned himself a God, stood with a kind of rare confidence. He seemed unmoved by anything but his own whims and desires. It's the kind of air that borders on madness, and tempts the ambitious to try their luck. No matter what you might think, no one could deny his grace, as he balanced effortlessly on the pool's raised edge. With one perfectly placed step at a time, Enki drew closer, all the while his gaze trained on the two children. His serpent's tongue flicked in and out, and the corners of his lips curled into a devious smile. It seemed the pomp and circumstance was a bit of a game, and it amused him. Finally, he stood, no more than a few meters away, and motioned for his servant to rise. Enki stretched out his hand and Isimud placed the timepieces in his master's open palm.

"I saw you in my dreams," Enki said, absentmindedly, twirling the watches on his finger. "It was ... a gift from the gods."

"Oh, yeah?" Zya asked innocently. "What did they show you?"

"Your intention," he said, nonchalantly. "To destroy me."

Elijah gasped but Zya wasn't fazed. She kept her calm and fired back. "Certainly, two little children wouldn't pose a threat to *you*, Oh, Lord of Earth."

"But you are not just children, are you?" he said, eyeing them intently as he played with Zya's timepiece. "Tell me, what does this do?"

"It's a timepiece, my Lord. It tells the time," Zya said.

"Time?" Enki said quizzically.

"Certainly, you're aware of the concept of time?" Elijah blurted out.

"Go on," Enki taunted. "Tell me, boy."

"Well," Elijah said, "Time, in its most fundamental form, is an unceasing rhythm that orchestrates the pattern of life. It's a result of Earth's rotation, our journey around the sun and humanity's constant striving to understand our place within the Universe."

"See," said Enki, stepping onto the pool's surface, and walking, one miraculous step at a time over the water. "That's the difference between you and I. Time does not apply to me. I am not confined by your infantile equations, nor can I be understood by your small-minded thinking. This is why I was born to rule and you were born to serve."

"Ssssooo wisssee." Isimud interjected.

"So," Zya said, "We should just ... do what you want because you're more evolved?"

"Precisely," Enki responded, with a look that almost indicated he was pleased with the question. "It puzzles me why so many fail to grasp this."

"Cause you're kind of being a bully," Elijah said.

Enki spun his head around, and sneered. "What did you say, boy?"

"He said," Zya snapped back, "You're acting like a bully ... and I happen to agree."

Isimud was on his feet in a flick of the tongue. "No one ssspeakssss to Massssterr like thattt."

Enki extended his hand in a gesture that said, *stand down*, and then turned back to the children.

"I know who you are," the Lord of Earth said. "*Guardians.*"

She stood still, shocked on the inside and stoic without. He knew who they were, had laid a perfect trap and was simply toying with them now. Still, Zya would not concede the high ground.

"If you know who we are, then you know that your days are numbered," she said. "This Empire will fall, and you with it. Leave now, take your soldiers with you, and you'll be spared."

Enki threw his head back, and let out a full-throated bellow that echoed through the chamber. "They didn't tell you what happened the last time, did they?"

"The last time?" Zya asked.

But Enki just smiled. "Eventually, little one, you'll learn your place."

Zya's eyes swelled with fire. "So, you think you can enslave my people, talk to me like I'm nobody and we're supposed to just accept it?"

"I couldn't have said it better myself," Enki mused with the air of a French king. "This is how it has always been, and will always be. It is ... *inevitable.*"

Zya laughed. "You think you're untouchable ..."

But he refused to acknowledge her response. "There's no shame in accepting what you are."

Her eyes narrowed. "... But you're not."

Zya and Enki stared each other down. The tension was so palpable that Elijah squirmed uncomfortably. Isimud hissed, ready to tear into them at his master's command. Then, out of nowhere, Enki's booming laugh broke the silence.

"I like your spirit, little girl. If you were one of us, well ... But you're *not* one of us."

He motioned behind them and two armored guards in lizard form — tongues, tails, talons and all — slinked out of the shadows and positioned themselves, one behind each of the children. They stood still, awaiting their orders.

"Now, you get to experience *real* power," Enki gloated, turning to the guards. "Take them away."

The guards shoved Zya and Elijah in their backs with electrified staves, sending an excruciating shock wave through their bodies. The Guardians winced with pain, as the sensation spread like a chain reaction, causing the very tips of their fingers and toes to feel like they were on fire. Worse yet, the spot on their skin where the staves made contact was still throbbing.

"The finessst room in the dungeon for the Guardiansss," Isimud said, with mock hospitality. "You'll be our guestsss of honor!"

CHAPTER EIGHT

Who Are You When the Lights Go Out?

They were in no position to resist, so the Guardians chose not to increase their pain. But they didn't give in, either. The guards prodded them anyway, seeming to delight in the agony they could inflict. The feeling was like nothing they'd ever experienced, and Zya imagined this is what torture was like. Excruciating. Unavoidable. Repeat. One foot in front of the other. *Don't let it break you.* Prod. Shock. *Don't let it get in your head.* Step, step, step. Prod. Shock. Repeat.

Don't let them win. Zya clenched her teeth tightly. It was all she could do to keep her head held high. She spotted Elijah in her periphery and could see the pain ripple across his face, too, but he did not cry out. And, so, they walked down flights of stairs, and more flights of stairs. And, the entire time, the Guardians kept their wits about them, until, with one last shove, the Archon guards pushed them into a dark, dank prison cell and swung the door closed with a "click".

"Jussst tryyy and get out of thisssss," they cackled.

And, like a hazy dream, the click-clack of the soldiers' claws disappeared into the darkness. Everything was black, except for one modestly burning torch that hung on the opposite wall and cast a soft, receding light just past the bars. Still disoriented from their gauntlet-walk, the children's eyes were slow to adjust, so they groped at the air to find each other. Elijah's hand landed on Zya's shoulder first, and once it was there, she took it and they embraced. It was a solemn, exhausted kind of hug, but one they needed, nonetheless.

Zya stepped back and held him at arm's length. "Are you alright?"

"I don't know if 'alright' is the word I'd use," he said. "I was pretty close to critical back there but I pulled it together around that last flight of stairs."

Zya smiled. "It's good to know you're still with me, old friend."

"Always," Elijah said.

And, even in that pitch black dungeon, they expertly executed their secret handshake.

"Still," Elijah wrinkled his nose, "It's not lookin' too good."

"I know," Zya responded softly. "But this isn't over yet."

"Um," he said, puzzled. "I'm not sure if you've noticed, but we're *locked up*. This isn't some movie, Zy ... it's not like the keys are hanging innocently on a hook across the room just waiting for us to grab them!"

"Just breathe," she said, taking a deep inhale.

Elijah followed suit, and they both let out a big sigh.

"There," she said. "How's that?"

"Well," Elijah said sardonically, "We're still locked up ... but at least I've achieved inner peace."

Zya shook her head, but she had a smile on her face. He always knew how to make her laugh. She tested the cell door, wishing it might, somehow, just fall right off its hinges. But it didn't budge. Not one bit.

"Search the perimeter," she said, pointing across the cell. "You start there, I'll start here and we can meet in the middle."

So, each of them traveled to the edge of the stone wall. The rock was damp and bumpy under their hands, with hills and valleys everywhere. They surveyed every inch, from the crease of the ground to as high as they could reach. But, by the time they came together, neither had found anything worth reporting.

Elijah shrugged his shoulders and let out a defeated sigh.

"Don't be like that," Zya said, making a face.

He sighed once more. This time, a little less dramatic-like. "It's just ... I don't know what to do."

"Me neither, Eli," Zya whispered. "I'm scared too, *okay?*"

"You're right," he said.

"Don't worry," she assured him. "We'll make it out eventually. We just need to put our heads together. We're gonna figure this out."

They stood face-to-face as they clasped their hands, right in right, and, left in left so that, from above, their interlocked arms looked like a giant "X". Though they would have been looking right at one another, they could barely see the face across from theirs. So they focused, instead, on the feeling of their friend's palm against theirs. Neither one uttered a peep, as they quieted their thoughts and dove deep, into the dark corners of their minds. They excavated every undiscovered crevice, hoping for a Hail Mary, a once-in-a-million shot to get out of this pickle. But they had no such luck.

Then, Zya felt something. She popped her awareness out of her thoughts and back into the physical realm, listened intently. There was nothing but silence. And, still, she was certain there was something else there. Zya put her finger to Eli's mouth and stood with him, as they silently held one another. At first, all they could hear was their own breathing. But, as they listened more closely, they started to pick up a low hum. The dripping of water. The crackling of the torch on the wall. And, as their ears became accustomed to the potpourri of sounds, they receded into the background. The humming, and the dripping, and the crackling were all still there, but, now, somehow, it was as if they could hear *through* them.

It was only once they'd centered themselves that the Guardians could hear another sound — a faint, but furious, sniffing. In fact, it was *so* quiet most would've written it off, lumping it in with the other white noise. But Zya wasn't just anyone. When the pitter-patter of tiny feet finally joined the symphony, her gut feeling was confirmed. Indeed, just a second or two later, a small desert mouse, almost exactly like the one they'd seen by the pyramids, appeared in the flickering light. It had a long, pink tail, with what looked like a paintbrush on top. A bouquet of long, thin whiskers hung so low at the ends that they seemed to tickle the ground. Its big, oval ears were slicked back and the hind legs looked long and powerful, like a kangaroo. They watched as a gecko, not much different than any little lizard you'd see in your own backyard, darted out of the shadows. It was just what the rodent was waiting for. And, with one lightning-quick jump, the desert mouse pounced on its prey, grabbing the reptile by its neck.

"Well, *that's* not strange," Elijah muttered.

Zya crouched down. "Where'd you come from, little guy?"

It was the kind of voice you might use with a child — inquisitive, and unassuming. Just as she said it, the mouse turned to look at them, and they could see the little lizard dangling between the rodent's teeth. With the mouse distracted, the gecko correctly identified its best chance of escape, and, giving a sharp kick, wriggled free, skittering off into a dark corner. The mouse, however, hadn't moved and Zya could swear it was looking straight at them. The children were even more surprised when the animal let out a series of angry squeaks, which, despite no direction from their universal translators, they could tell they were being admonished. And by this tiny little thing, no less.

Zya spoke again. "Are you trying to tell us something?"

The tiny creature let out one more high-pitched squeak and, then, in the next moment, seemed to be growing. Because of the low light, the children weren't sure, at first, if it was their eyes playing tricks on them or not. But they'd already dealt with so many strange surprises it didn't seem like one more would be too much trouble. Besides, whatever was happening didn't feel dangerous, not like before. You know, that feeling of deep uneasiness just before something's about to go sideways? It wasn't there. In fact, they were, surprisingly, at ease.

The tiny mouse was no longer tiny, and it was also no longer a mouse. Instead, in the place where the erstwhile rodent once stood, was now a small boy, of maybe eight or nine years old. He had a pair of wild chestnut eyes, set under arched jet-black eyebrows, and his skin was the color of rust and chocolate. A tattered, sand-colored shirt hung from his wiry shoulders and, around his waist, a pair of brown knee-high pants, no doubt made by the hand of some native mother. He was skinny, but athletic, with nothing but muscle on his bones.

At this point, the Guardians didn't know what to expect. After all, this was the second being they'd seen transform before their eyes, and both in just the last hour. At least this one wasn't holding them prisoner. In fact, it might've been that they were meeting in this cell, but the little guy already felt more trustworthy. Still, Zya was skeptical. *Nothing is what it seems*, she thought, determined to get to the truth.

The boy spoke with a soft voice. "They didn't hurt you, did they?"

"No," Elijah said. "Well, not *too* much."

"The electro-staves hurt," he said.

Zya knelt down, placing her hands gently on the little boy's shoulders, and gazed inquisitively into his deep, dark eyes. "What did they do to *you*?"

"They take something different every day," he said.

"How did you do that?" Elijah chimed in. "I mean ... you were ... a mouse."

"You aren't from here, are you?" Asked the little boy.

"No," Zya answered. "We're not."

"And you *can't* change?"

The children looked at each other.

"No," Zya said. "This is what we look like."

"But you can move from place to place," he said. "Without even trying."

They looked at each other again, confused.

"I saw you running from the Fiends," he said, in a voice that almost sounded like a squeak. "In the shantytown, under the pyramid."

"So it *was* you!" Elijah exclaimed.

The boy nodded.

"Oh," Zya said, "You're talking about the jumping. We need our timepieces for that. Enki took them."

At the mention of the ruler's name, the little boy gasped and a sudden hush descended over the room. Just as the silence fell, they could hear the jangling of keys. It was coming down the hall, along with the click-clacking claws of the Archon guards. And it was getting closer.

"Why would they be back so soon?" Zya whispered.

"This *can't* be good." Elijah said.

"Quick," said the boy. "Hide!"

Elijah grabbed Zya by the hand and she followed him into the deepest, darkest corner, as their ally returned to his shrew state and ducked behind a prison bar, not a foot from the cell door.

And, so, they waited, in breathless silence.

CHAPTER NINE

Two Is Good, Three Is Better

The guards stepped out of the corridor and into the room, scales shimmering as the light bounced off their reptilian hides. There was something in them that looked wild. It might have been the eyes. With only a sliver of iris, it was eerie when they blinked. *They really do move like Velociraptors*, Zya thought, their heads bobbing with each step, and the same opposable claw on their back legs, right where a thumb would be. Their visages had a kind of resting-slimeball-face, where they always seemed to be up to something devious. The corners of their mouths even seemed to naturally curl up in a scheming smile.

"The Lord mussst have ssomething ssspecial in mind for our prisonersss," said the slightly bigger one.

"It musst be important for the general to call for them sso sssoon," the other said, gleefully.

A bolt of fear shivered down Zya's neck, and she could feel Elijah's grip tighten. *How're we gonna get outta this?* she wondered, squeezing Elijah's hand back. Then, she noticed their little friend, surreptitiously scurrying up the prison bars toward the lock, where the Archons, fully oblivious to the designs of the little creature, were fumbling with the keys.

"Where arrre youuu?" the beefy one sneered, as they waited anxiously to rough up the Guardians again.

Just then, the key clicked in the lock and the door swung open. Without any hesitation, the mouse made his move. Scurrying over the handle, he leapt at the arm of the one closest to him and, digging in, scaled up its shoulder. Stunned, the Archon guard let out a cry and tried to swat the fleet-footed pest. But the rodent was quick, and the guard was disoriented, and, rather than thwart his attacker, he connected squarely with his partner, instead.

This was the opening they needed. Zya rose and, pulling Elijah by the hand, ran for the door. The guards were so preoccupied with the little troublemaker — he was currently zig-zagging down the back of the one nearest the door — that, at first, they didn't even notice the children. This miniature distraction was running quite the interference. The Archon who'd been hit, furiously tried to connect with the rodent, swinging his electro-staff, in an effort to end the little fella for good. But, every time he swung, the little critter cut a "Z", causing the Archon to miss. So, there they were, the two guards, one hopping around and swatting at himself, while the other landed electrified strikes on his friend. Even in the midst of the action, Zya wondered whether the beating was a genuine mistake, or simply payback for that first, misplaced strike. Either way, the disturbance was working wonders.

The children burst through the cell door and, before they'd taken a step, were forced to let each other go, in order to avoid a face-full of electro-staff. Elijah sidestepped the first guard, who was still trying to brush the little troublemaker off his hide. The second guard seemed to consider chasing after Elijah but elected, instead, to turn, blocking Zya's escape. She was square in his sights, and all her alarm bells were ringing. She had to make a quick decision, and she did. In fact, it felt like a reflex, an instinct, if you will. Zya hit the floor running, perfectly splitting the legs of the Archon guard. Once she was through, she angled her rubber soles down so they hit the floor again, popping her back to her feet in a flash. Some four or five meters down the hall, Elijah stood still, a look of concerned surprise covering his face.

"Go!" she yelled. "Go, go, go!"

By the time he snapped out of it, she was right on his tail, and the guards were right behind her. They tore through the hallways, around corners and up flights of stairs, retracing their steps to the Throne Room. At one point, they could hear the sound of paws running beside them and were happy to know their little friend was still there. But the guards were big, and angry, and they knew these corridors inside and out. Unfortunately for the lizards, the twisting halls and slick floors were a great equalizer. They slipped and slid around each and every turn, and the Guardians took notice, using it to their advantage. So, by the skin of their tennis shoes, the children were able to stay just enough ahead.

At one point, Zya could feel, very distinctly, the breeze of a swipe, and imagined the guards' long, sharp claws slashing mere millimeters from her neck. There was more than one close call, but they continued on unharmed. Eventually, their little friend took the lead and the children, giving every last effort they had, screeched around the final turn and, bouncing off the wall, burst into the open. The Guardians, hearing a series of high-pitched squeaks, looked up to see their timepieces resting, unguarded, on the arm of Enki's throne.

As they booked a beeline across the room, what seemed like wave after wave of Archon guards emerged from the shadows. It was as if the sides of two great oceans were closing in on them. But Zya could see the way, and pushed forward, sprinting up the stairs, with her compatriots close behind. She found another gear, as the palace guards hissed at their heels, reaching the throne just in time to toss Elijah his timepiece. It was a perfect exchange, and he slipped the watch on, just as one of the guards lunged at him. And, like that, he was next to her.

"Let's do this," she said, with a smirk.

They shared a cheeky look, as the Archons closed in, clawing up the stairs at their master's throne. And, just as they were within arm's length, the children disappeared. The wave of guards came to a halt, looking about in disbelief. And, then, they reappeared, right in the middle of the crowd. The next half-minute was pandemonium as the Guardians jumped in and out like guerilla fighters, landing blow after blow on the confused and overmatched guards. Zya appeared behind one, and crippled his leg with a kick to the knee. At the very same time, Elijah materialized on top of a sideways electro-staff and landed a punch to the lizard's long jaw. They looked like lighting, and moved like ghosts.

Again, a hysterical squeaking grabbed the Guardians' attention and they looked up to see their little friend heading toward a crack in the wall. He went for the crease, and the children followed, jumping out of the scrum as the Archons, rabid at their humiliation, followed, like a school of fish. With one last chorus, their ally disappeared through the opening and, a moment later, Elijah was squeezing in too. It was a tight fit, even for him, as he inched, bit by bit, toward safety.

"Go, go, go," Zya exclaimed, hitting the hole at top speed.

A medley of hands, fingers and claws reached out, in unison, and grabbed at the opening. A long reptilian claw caught the end of Zya's jacket, but the children sucked in their stomachs, refusing defeat, and popped out the other side.

"You won't essscapee," one of the guards hissed through the crack.

"Masssterr will get youuu," said another. "Iffff you ever get outtt."

But they were too big to fit through, so all they could do now was issue idle threats. Suddenly, the armed guards didn't seem as scary as before. Honestly, they just sounded bitter, like a vindictive friend or lover wishing you ill. All the excitement and anxiety of the chase was gone, but for a bit of heavy breathing. Of the two, Elijah was slightly more winded. Although, in retrospect, he was surprised he'd been able to keep up as well as he did.

Elijah put his arms out to each side and his hands met rock. The walls were narrow on both sides. By the small sliver of light coming through the crack behind him, Eli could see Zya in front of him, peering cautiously into the darkness. The void was vast, like a big black hole, endlessly, all-encompassing nothingness. Elijah wouldn't admit it to anyone — even his very best friend — but he was still scared of the dark. It was the thing he'd hated most, as a little boy. Not so much the darkness itself, but the unknown of it, the morbid mystery of what might be lurking within. Between the cell and, now, this tunnel, it was like a very real nightmare.

"Anything else," he muttered. "It could've been anything else."

"Huh?" Zya asked.

"Oh, nothing," Elijah said, dismissively. "It's just ... you'd think these watches would have a flashlight or something."

"Eli!" Zya's face lit up. "Maybe they do!"

She started fiddling with the dials and, as she twisted and turned them, once again, she heard the voice of Grandma Anita. *Breathe, baby. Just breathe. And don't you forget, I'm always with you.* She stopped trying, and let her arms fall to her side, closing her eyes to take a deep breath. Then, without any effort, the face of the watch came to life with a light so bright it shocked their eyes at first.

"Just *think* it," she said to her friend. "The same way we jump."

Elijah followed her lead and his timepiece illuminated, as well. Suddenly, the corridor, which had been so dark and foreboding just moments before, was flooded with a great luminance, and they breathed a sigh of relief. They'd still have to tread lightly but, at least, now, there was hope.

CHAPTER TEN

The three children walked silently through the pitch black, guided only by the light of their magical watches and the nose of their furry companion. The light only extended about fifty feet in both directions, but it was something. After all the commotion, the quiet darkness was actually relieving. It felt like a blanket on Zya's mind. Even so, she couldn't stop thinking about everything that had happened. They'd traveled through time, found themselves on an alien spaceship, been given magic watches and seen the Pyramids for the first time. They were captured, interrogated, tortured and escaped from prison with the help of a new friend. But they couldn't stop now. They had to keep going, and with a big target on their back, no less. No one knew exactly what Enki had planned for them, but they knew it wouldn't be good. The path ahead was uncertain, but that uncertainty was better than anything behind them, for sure. No inventor has ever said the risk is too great. In fact, being willing to risk it all for the hope of something greater is the mark of a true leader.

"Hey," Zya said, to their new ally. "Thanks for all your help back there. I doubt we'd have made it without you."

"Anything for a Guardian," he said meekly.

"How?" Elijah said.

The skinny native boy pointed to the timepiece. "Guardians are the only ones who have *those*."

"There are more of us?" Zya asked.

"We have stories," he said. "The wise men have prophesied the return of the Guardians for hundreds of years, and say it will spell our freedom."

"What's your name, anyway?" Zya asked.

"Said." The little boy sounded it out for them a second time, emphasizing every syllable. "Sai-eed."

"Nice to meet you, Said," she said, "I'm Zya."

Then, she gestured toward her friend.

"Elijah," he added, right on cue. "My friends call me Eli."

"It is an honor to meet you, Zya," he nodded. "Eli."

"Do you know where we are?" she asked.

"These are the catacombs," he said. "Usually, no one comes down here."

"Why not?"

"Ghost stories," he responded. "Mothers tell bedtime stories about undead pharaohs, ancient artifacts and dark magic. That's enough to keep most of us away."

Elijah's eyes got big. "*Zombies*?!"

"They're probably just old wives tales," Zya assured him. "Besides, did you even *hear* the other part? 'Ancient artifacts'?"

Elijah raised an eyebrow.

"Does this mean something to you?" Said asked.

Zya turned to him. "We've been sent here to find a device of immense power that we're told is the key to defeat the Archons."

Now, it was Said's turn to look surprised. "So, the prophecies are true, then."

Suddenly, he fell to a knee and bowed his head. Zya and Elijah looked at each other, confused.

"None of that, now," Zya said, as she brought him back to his feet. "We're not here to rule you, we're here to set you free."

In reverence, Said traced a cross over his head and heart. "I will do whatever I can to aid you, noble Guardians. Just say the word."

Zya patted Said on the shoulder. "It's good to know we can count on you, friend."

"So," said Elijah. "Are there any stories about where we might find this ancient artifact?"

"Wellll," Said stroked his chin. "I might know where to look."

"I thought you said no one comes down here?" Elijah inquired.

"I said *most of us*," he shot back. "I've never been one to follow the rules too closely."

"So, you know where it is, then?" Zya asked expectantly.

"Not exactly," Said responded. "I never came across anything like that. But there's a bunch of tunnels under the Pyramids I haven't explored yet."

Elijah nodded vigorously. "There's a bunch of temples over there, too. No better place to hide an artifact."

"There was one wing in particular," Said recalled. "It was cold."

Zya and Elijah looked at each other.

"Cold?" she asked.

"Cold," he nodded. "Cold enough to keep most away."

"Can you lead us there?"

"Of course," Said explained. "It's a bit of a hike, though."

Elijah shrugged, so Zya turned back to their guide. "Sounds like our best option. Are you sure you can get us there?"

His face became very serious. "We will succeed, or die trying."

"Uh, if at all possible," Elijah interjected, "Let's avoid the latter."

CHAPTER ELEVEN

The Night is Darkest Before the Dawn

The low light of an oil lamp cast a soft shadow over a solid oak desk, the top of which was littered with maps. They had strange names like "Woolsthorpe Manor, Lincolnshire, England, 1665", "Athens, Greece, 363 BCE", "Vedic India" and another simply titled "The New World". But, most eye-catching of all, on the very top, an ornately drawn document that seemed, even in context of the others, to be ancient. It depicted a beautiful circular metropolis, consisting of a sizable central island, surrounded by four progressively larger rings — two of land, and two of water. It was made from a thicker, more durable material than the others and, scrawled across the top, in a stunningly beautiful script, the words, "The Kingdom of Atlantis".

In the middle of the room, Enki lay, in a dreamless sleep, in the middle of a vaulted-frame, gold-studded bed. His chest rose and fell, as the purple curtains and soft white veil rippled lightly with the evening breeze. Suddenly, breaking the peaceful silence, the door burst open, and Isimud shuffled in. Breathing frantically and sweating through his scales, he stood nervously at the edge of the bed, and spoke to his master in a sheepish tone.

"Highnesss," he said. "*Highnesss?*"

Enki opened his eyes and glared at his sniveling advisor. "Why do you disturb me at this ungodly hour?"

"Highnesss," he repeated again, as if uncertain of whether he could actually say what came next. "The children are gone."

Enki sat up with a start. "How could this be?"

"They had an accomplissss," the general hissed, bowing his head ever so slightly and hunching himself over, so as to make as small a target as possible. "A Brotherhood sssspy."

Enki's eyes narrowed and he was out of bed at once, as servants, patiently waiting just outside, streamed in to do their master's bidding.

"Contact every agent we have," he barked. "I want to know where they're headed before they do."

"Yesss, massster," he said, and, with the wave of a hand, dispatched his own agent to carry out the order.

"At least we have their magical watches," Enki sighed.

"Well," Isimud bowed his head even lower.

"Yes?" Enki clenched his teeth.

"... You ... uh, they were left on your throne," Isimud said. "During their essscapeee the children reclaimed the devisssesss and decimated the Royal Guard."

The Lizard King bit his tongue. "I'll deal with them myself."

Enki stood in front of a full-length mirror as his servants — all humans — dressed him in a titanium battle suit, complete with a helmet that fit perfectly over the horned crown. As the helmet slid into place, an advisor shuffled into the room, whispering in Isimud's ear before shuffling back out.

"Masssterr," started the schemer. "We've detected a sssub-space disssturbansss in orbit."

"Concentrate a Chroniton Beam at it," Enki ordered. "Flush them out."

"Yesssssir," Isimud nodded, bowing his head as he started to leave. But, as the rest of the servants departed, the Lord of Earth motioned for him to stay.

"What isss itt, Masssterr?"

Enki clenched his teeth. "The Lumerians. They're here for the tablets."

"It'sss reassonable to think ssso, My Lord," Isimud hissed. "They may be the reassson for the children, as well."

"My loyal servant, you are correct," said the Lizard King. "There's *something* about them."

"They have been quite a nuisssance, my liege." Isimud smiled deviously. "I hope, for your sssake, the prophessy doess not come true."

"Prophecy?" Enki asked, surprised.

"Their old men sssay the arrival of two young ssaviorsss will ssspell their freedom."

The god-king eyed his general with suspicion. "Why am I only hearing of this now?"

"How wasss I to know, My Lord?" Isimud pouted. "It ssseemed far-fetched, to think children would pose any danger. "

"In that, you are also correct, my servant," Enki mused. "And, yet, I am not one to take the power of a prophecy for granted. At least, it could be used to embolden the people."

Enki walked over to the wall and, through a skinny window-slit, surveyed his domain. The sky was just starting to brighten and the sun bathed everything in sight — the lush gardens, the city outside, the great river and the pyramids behind it — in the light of early morning. Best of all, it was *his*, and he intended to keep it that way.

Enki turned to Isimud with a look of determination in his eyes. "I want to know where those children are within the hour. And, once the Lumerians are exposed, take them down."

"So shall it be written," said the smarmy general, taking a bow. "So shall it be done."

CHAPTER TWELVE

The Guardians had nothing left to do but trust this scrawny native boy, and so they did, following him through tunnel after tunnel, after tunnel. Lots and lots of tunnels. The circumstance would have induced panic in most. And, while they had the benefit of the light from Zya and Elijah's watches, it was almost as if they were buried in one, big, neverending tomb. It was stuffy, and damp, and, to the naked eye, there was no sign that any particular direction was any better than the other. Said would periodically switch between forms, in order to remember the way, or sniff it out with his rodent nose. This way, they pushed deeper, and deeper, and the air became thicker, and thicker, until it felt like they were stealing every breath.

"Goodness," Elijah exclaimed. "What's that smell?"

"These tunnels are connected to a bunch of tombs," Said explained. "Back, before the Archons came, we buried our dead down here."

"Well," Elijah said. "That explains it."

They reached a fork in the road, two paths that led in diverging directions, one to the right and the other to the left. Yet again, Said returned to his diminutive form, sniffing loudly into each tunnel, and surveying the ground before them, as he worked to uncover any sign that might help them find their way.

"This way," he finally said, pointing.

"So, you can change ... like the Archons?" Elijah asked.

"It's how I was born," Said answered. "It's how we're all born. Some are just more ... attuned."

"How does it work?"

Said gestured to their timepieces. "How does *that* work?"

"You, kind of, just imagine where you want to go, and it takes you there."

"Well," he said. "It's kind of like that. I just envision myself as one or the other and I *become* it."

"Can you turn into anything else?" Zya asked.

Said was silent for a moment. "I've never tried."

Elijah's mouth nearly fell off its hinges. "Never tried?!"

"Alsaghir, the desert mouse, was the first animal I saw, and I imprinted on him," Said explained. "So is the way."

"But," Elijah asked. "*Could* you?"

"They say our ancestors could change at will," he explained. "That they could become whatever they wanted. But, it's different now."

"What do you mean?" Zya asked.

"People are afraid," he said. "Most children usually still imprint, but they lose it around six or seven."

"Then, how come you still can?" Elijah asked.

"You lose the ability to change when you accept the way things are," he said. "And, I simply cannot."

"Why not?"

Said clenched his teeth, and let out a big sigh. "They took my family."

They stopped, and there was nothing but silence. Silence, and their shallow breathing. Silence, and the light in the dark. Silence.

Finally, Zya spoke in a whisper. "I'm so sorry."

"It's my pain to bear," Said responded.

"What happened?" Elijah asked.

"Elijahhh!" Zya landed a perfectly placed elbow between his ribs, eliciting a screech.

"Hey! What was that for?"

"Be *polite*," she said, teeth clenched.

"It's okay," Said jumped in. "You deserve to know. It was the Harvest Festival, last year. After the parade, there's a ceremony at the palace where everybody presents their 'offerings'. It makes me sick just thinking about it."

Zya placed her hand on his shoulder. "You don't have to say any more."

"Yes," Said replied. "Yes, I do. You need to know."

He stopped and turned to both of them. "For the final sacrifice, they always select a young child."

"And, *then* what?" Elijah asked, horrified.

"We assume the worst," Said replied.

"Children?" Zya exclaimed.

"Anyone under the age of four is eligible," he explained. "It was my sister's last year. She got picked, and my father fell apart. He tried to convince them not to take her, so they vaporized him on the spot. After that, the Brotherhood found me, and taught me how to be a rebel."

Said closed his eyes, bowing his head, and they could feel the sadness inside him. Zya wished that, somehow, she could take it all away. And, she also knew that the pain was a part of him, so she wouldn't try to take that from him, at all. But, maybe she could ease his burden, free his mind a little. She stepped forward, finding his eyes and holding his head in her hands.

"It's not your fault," she said. "It's not your fault they were killed, and it's not your fault you couldn't do anything about it. But we're gonna stop them now."

Said gazed back at her with a look that said, "Please let it be true," as one single, solitary teardrop escaped his eye. But there was also a smile on his face.

"Bless you," he said. "Because of you, we have hope."

CHAPTER THIRTEEN

Lions and Tigers and Bears, Oh My!

They continued together through the dark in silence. Everything that needed to be said had been said and it was safer this way, since there was no telling what was around the corner. A draft of cool, dank air hit Zya smack in the face, and the little company stopped cold. They could see a faint glow coming from ahead, as the tunnel appeared to widen slightly. And, yet, an air of apprehension hung in the space between them. Zya stepped forward first, motioning for the others to follow. As they pushed forward, it got colder, and colder. *At least we're on the right track*, Zya thought. But it was so cold now that Said's teeth started to chatter and the three of them, in their thin, summer clothes, began to shiver. Zya, who had the benefit of her jacket, put her arm around Eli on one side and Said on the other, and they held each other close to ration the warmth. The rag-tag group held on for dear life as they plodded forward, focusing on each and every breath to keep from going crazy.

"Howww mmuch ffartherrr?" Elijah asked, shivering like an earthquake.

"Nnnott muchhh," Said said, pointing ahead, and they could see that the light was growing. It was getting brighter.

"Stay with me," Zya said, pulling her compatriots even closer. They continued forward, in unison, one step at a time. As they approached the opening, they could see that, indeed, the walls of the tunnel parted, causing the stone hallway to double in width. As they inched closer, it became clear that the light peeking out of the darkness had a tinge of color to it. They drew nearer and nearer, and the light grew, enveloping them in its bright green glow. In fact, they didn't need their watches to light the way anymore. It was even getting warmer, as if a great source of heat was competing with the cold, and beating it back. The light enveloped everything and, as they got closer, seemed to pulsate softly, like a beating heart.

Apprehensive yet determined, Zya stepped through, pulling the others with her. In one big stride, they crossed the threshold into a circular, dome-like cave that resembled a hollowed-out half-circle. The ceiling was tall at its apex, measuring at least twenty feet at the highest point, a stark contrast to the cramped hall from which they'd just emerged. Four rock formations jutted out of the otherwise-smooth walls, creating the illusion of corners, though, in reality, there were none. A path, made of red stone, cut and laid through the middle of the room, ended in front of what looked like an altar.

The big, rectangular block of smooth jet-black granite jutted out of the earth as if it had something to say. But this was just the appetizer. Propped on top was the source of the light itself: two dark green, see-through, table-thick tablets. Emanating from deep inside the tablets, the sacred light bathed the cavern in an ominous viridescence, convincing Zya, without a doubt, of what she already knew — these were the Emerald Tablets. Something inside them seemed to call to her, echoing deep within her being. *What was this?* She could feel an invisible force pulling her toward them. They whispered seductively in her ear, egging her forward.

"Reach out and touch me," the soft voice whispered. "You know you want to."

They were right — she *did* want to. It was the first time anyone had spoken to her like this, and it felt different than the orders she usually got. This voice was inviting, and it ignited the curiosity within her. She wanted, so badly, to see for herself, that it didn't seem to register that the voice wanted it too. She felt a part of herself awaken, a desire at her very core. And, even though she knew she probably shouldn't, she wanted to anyway.

Somewhere along the way, she'd let go of Eli and Said, who were standing just inside the entrance in a bit of a trance themselves. Zya crept ahead, mesmerized by the emerald glow. It was exhilarating, how the voice made her feel special, how it made her feel wanted and unique. The voice came from an even deeper place than the word of a Lumerian, and it genuinely felt as if the tablets were speaking to her, and her alone. When they spoke to her, she mattered, in a way she didn't even know that she needed. And, at one point, though Zya thought she could hear Elijah calling her, she ignored his muffled warnings.

He probably wants the tablets for himself, Zya thought. Either way, it was too late. The voice in her head drowned out everything else and, having given in to her selfish desire, she found herself at the mercy of the tablets. Zya reached out her hand, and everything else started to fade. All she could see was the green, green glow, and all she wanted was to hold them in her arms and feel the power. Finally, she would have what she'd always wanted. Then, just as she reached out, Zya felt a hand on her shoulder. It was heavy and she was sure it was Elijah, but she couldn't stop now. She was helpless to resist. And, as he tried to pull her back, the tip of Zya's finger grazed the face of the tablets, tracing what looked like a giant scar, from corner to corner. As her finger disconnected, she snapped out of the hypnotic trance.

"Are you okay?" Elijah asked.

Zya shook her head to clear the cobwebs. "I think so."

"What happened?" he asked. "I was trying to call you, but it was like you couldn't hear me or something."

"I don't know," she said, looking down at her hands. "The tablets, they were talking to me like they wanted ..."

Cutting Zya off mid-sentence, the rock formation behind them began to crumble. They watched, spellbound, as a face emerged. But it wasn't the face of a man, or even that of an Archon. No, it was the head of a jackal, black as the midnight sky, with a long, sharp snout and pointy ears. The monstrosity was massive, almost ten feet if Elijah was right. Finally, it shook the last of the rubble off like dust, revealing the body of a strongly built man. Wrapped around its hips, the shendyt of a pharaoh, and draped over its muscular chest and shoulders, an ornate collar. But the skin, no doubt flawless in a former life, had turned a pallid yellow, and large patches of rotting flesh were falling off the corpse.

"So, *that's* where the smell's coming from," Elijah exclaimed, pinching his nose.

Hearing the sound, the head snapped around, and beady jackal eyes stared down the two children. It was as if the monster was looking straight through them, and the big black irises were windows to a bottomless pit. They were so bloodshot and yellowed that barely any white was left. It was like looking at the face of Death, and Death was onto them. It picked up one leg, bending at the knee just enough to slide its foot over the ground, and fell forward, again and again, in what looked like controlled chaos. It might take a while, but there was no doubt it was coming for them.

Elijah's eyes got big. "Zya."

She grabbed at the tablets, shaking them back-and-forth, in a futile attempt to dislodge the artifact. In fact they wouldn't budge one bit. *What is this, some kind of King Arthur, Sword-in-the-Stone-type fairy tale?* Zya thought. Even if it was, the tablets had called to her. So, why were they being so gosh darn stubborn now? The undead pharaoh took another lumbering step, and another, rattling the cave with each advance.

"Just perfect," she muttered, trying the tablets once more.

This time, Elijah's voice was noticeably more agitated. "*Zyaaa!*"

She looked up just in time to see the undead pharaoh swipe at her friend.

"No!" She screamed.

Zya reached out, in that way that you might if your friend was about to be hurt, and you were standing right there watching, but couldn't do anything to stop it. Elijah was quick, though, and, just before the zombie hand could grab him, he jumped to safety. Zya felt a surge of anger within her, and reacting reflexively, went on the offensive. She jumped to within an inch of those jackal teeth and, with a growl of her own, unleashed a roundhouse kick on the zombie's snout. But, as she tried to jump away, Zya found herself falling instead.

She spotted Elijah and could see his eyes wide as headlamps. His lips were moving, too. She couldn't decipher what he was saying, but she didn't have to. She could feel it, herself. Something was wrong with the timepiece. It wasn't spinning up. In fact, she thought it might be cooling down still. Next, though, rather than falling, she felt a cold, hard hand catch her around the wrist and Zya felt herself get yanked up, until she was eye-to-eye with the monster. It growled, and she growled back. The eyes were even more terrifying up close. They were crazy. They were mad. It was like staring into a calm pool and a furious storm at the same time, which made the whole thing even more terrifying. Plus, it didn't help matters that, now, being so close to the thing, Zya could *actually* smell the rotting flesh, and it was worse than she'd imagined.

With the other hand, it grabbed her around the waist, glaring into her eyes. Its grip was cold as ice, and she realized the sub-zero temperatures were coming from the creature itself. In fact, the intense cold was probably the reason it hadn't rotted completely. All of a sudden, a look of fury came into its eyes and it tossed Zya across the room like a rag doll. She hurtled through the air, careening toward an especially pointy rock formation, and tried, once more, to teleport to safety. This time, the timepiece came to life, and, just barely spinning up in time, dropped her beside her best friend.

Elijah ran to her side. "Are you okay?"

"Cold," Zya blurted out. "It's cold, and it's slowing everything down."

"Yeah," he said. "I'm pretty sure that's Anubis."

She looked at him confused.

"The Egyptian god of the underworld."

"Well," Zya cracked. "At least it's on-brand."

"What do we do?" Elijah's voice was anxious, as the undead deity lumbered toward them again.

"Shhhhh," she said. "Let me think."

Zya closed her eyes, and took a deep breath, silencing her mind. She focused on the moment and everything slowed — it was as if she was *inside* her breath, rather than *doing* the breathing. She was being carried by the air itself, like a surfer on a wave. Zy could feel every inch of the cave, as the zombie god bore down on them. Suddenly, her eyes opened in a flash, and she looked up. The movement was so small it hardly registered at first. On the rocky outcropping behind Elijah, resting on a large boulder, was their little whiskered friend, trying to get their attention like his life depended on it.

Zya turned to Eli. "Go, help him."

"I can't leave you here," he said.

She grabbed him by the shoulders. "I need you to trust me. I'll draw him in, and you finish it. Now, go!"

Elijah shook his head, reluctantly, and jumped to the ledge. As the stones materialized in front of Eli, Said climbed down from the rock and transformed back into a little boy. The two young lads gave each other a quick look of acknowledgement and started to push. Back on the ground, Zya was playing the role of bait with enthusiasm. Sure, maybe her timepiece wasn't working like normal, but that didn't mean she was totally defenseless. Eventually, she found her way to a spot underneath the outcropping and dug in the heels of her red Converse All-Stars. Her nostrils flared, as she showed her teeth and claws, crouched in an athletic stance. Anubis took another heavy step and let out an animalistic wail that made the hair on Zya's neck stand up. Its eyes were burning a bright green, which made the thing look even scarier.

The two young boys threw their bodies against the rock, but it wouldn't budge. Elijah looked in Said's eyes, and could see that his panting counterpart was similarly discouraged regarding the odds of success, given their current strategy. In other words, they weren't gonna get it to move. A wave of terror coursed through Elijah, as he looked down at his friend. Anubis was nearly on top of her now. She needed him, but he didn't know what to do. All he knew is that he didn't want her to get hurt and he'd have to figure something out. Elijah's mind went to work, synapses firing like little nuclear explosions, and it seemed as if he was receiving a download. Indeed, he came to with an idea. *This has to work*, he thought. *Trust yourself, Elijah.*

"Any *time*!" Zya yelled.

"Step back," he said, waving Said away from the boulder.

"*No-ow*," Zya said, in that agitated, sing-song-y kind of tone a mother might use on a child who hadn't done their chores.

"Here goes nothin'," he mumbled.

Eli extended his hands toward the boulder like he was trying to use The Force on it and, after a moment or two of struggling, took a deep breath. The giant stone disappeared, as if it had never been there, at all, and, less than a second later, re-materialized directly over the spot where Zya was standing. At that very moment, the undead pharaoh lunged for Zya again and, this time, she timed the jump perfectly, just as he grasped at her throat. And, for a second, it seemed like Anubis was frozen, reaching for the empty space where Zya had been, as the boulder hung over its head. There was no escape, now. Down, down, down, gravity worked its magic, dropping the enormous stone square on the zombie's head.

CHAPTER FOURTEEN

Two Steps Forward, One Step Back

Just off the main bridge of the Nimrod, inside the captain's waiting room, Maroun sat, with impeccable posture, in a tall-backed swiveling chair. Behind him, hundreds of stars sparkled confidently outside the large bay window. He sat at a console desk, smack in the middle of the room, which looked like someone had taken a stick of gum and bent it down on both sides, until it touched the floor. The console was made of shatter-proof glass and, on its face, displayed captain's logs, crew manifests and other communications.

The Lumerian captain was reading a report — off another, smaller screen — of their recent attempts to pinpoint the children's location. The timepieces should have made it easy for the Nimrod to find them, but scans had been blank for the last few hours. They should have been able to pick up the Guardians' signatures anywhere on the surface, which meant they were either in hiding, had been captured and were being held or ... the unthinkable had happened. Though Maroun was working earnestly, his face did not betray it. He needed to keep a steady hand, so that he would not be swayed by emotion. The entire crew, and the children on the planet's surface, were counting on him. It was his duty to be a rock, and inspire those around him to rise to the challenge. The only acceptable outcome was success, and so, he would act accordingly. Indeed, as a veteran of tense situations, Maroun was well aware there was no telling what would tilt the balance. So, he could not rest.

A soft sound rippled from the direction of the door.

"Come in," Maroun responded.

It was Kelven. "Sir."

"Yes?" Maroun said.

"We were able to trace a series of temporal disturbances to the Archon palace," the first officer reported.

"The timepieces."

"Precisely, sir. It looks like there was some kind of commotion, and, then, they disappeared."

"What do you mean *disappeared?*" Maroun asked.

"Exactly that, sir," they said. "There was a cluster of localized activity, over the course of a couple minutes and, after that ... absolutely nothing."

"Is it possible the timepieces could have been vaporized?" Maroun asked.

"Possible, sir? Yes," Kelven answered. "Likely? Those watches are nearly indestructible."

"When did this all happen?"

"Twenty-one hundred," they answered.

Maroun lowered his screen. "Let us pray all is not lost."

"With all due respect, sir, all is never lost," Kelven assured him.

They'd been captain and first mate for nearly two thousand cycles, and Kelven had learned much from the wise and experienced Lumerian. He had immense respect for the accomplished explorer and knew that uncertainty is the price one pays for blazing a trail. No one was more calm under pressure than Maroun. Just then, an impact surged through the ship like an earthquake. And two more tremors, in quick succession.

"To the bridge!" Maroun ordered.

The duo stumbled through the door and onto the main bridge, just as another shot hit home.

"Report!"

"We've sustained damage to the hull," the helmsman yelled over the alarms. "High energy weapon, originating on the surface."

"The Archons," Kelven said.

"Activate the deflector," Maroun ordered. "Take us to the other side of the moon."

"They found us," Kelven stated. "But, how?"

"It looks like they used a wave of Chroniton particles to penetrate our cloak," the helmsman responded.

"Clever," Maroun muttered.

"It must have avoided our sensor sweeps," said Kelven, "since Chroniton particles can be naturally occurring."

"Full stop on the far side of Earth's moon, sir," the helmsman reported.

"Good," Maroun said. "Maintain position."

"But, sir," Kelven said. "We're out of transporter range."

"We won't be able to help them at all if we get shot down," Maroun said coolly.

Kelven bowed their head. "Of course, sir."

"We'll take the risk when it matters." Maroun advised. "Monitor the planet for any activity and keep me apprised."

CHAPTER FIFTEEN

The Only Way Is Through

The boulder landed on the undead pharaoh with a *crunch*, breaking limbs and crushing its face to smithereens. At first, they were skeptical it was over, but the boulder had found its new home, and that home just happened to have a pancaked zombie underneath it.

There's nothing quite like a good hug in the immediate aftermath of a traumatic event. In fact, it feels like the natural response. So the new little band of friends engaged in a cathartic embrace. As their heartbeats settled back to normal, they could feel the bond they had for one another grow even deeper. Sometimes, it was easy for Zya to forget how much she needed other people. In fact, if it was up to her, she wouldn't need anyone. But, as it was, these two weren't bad, and she felt stronger with them all pulling together. At no point was this more evident than now, as they hooted and hollered, smiling wide and tugged at each other's shoulders.

"You did it!" Zya exclaimed. "How did you do that?"

"I have no idea," Elijah remarked, still surprised, himself.

"Well, it worked!" she responded. "And, you ..."

She bent down to a knee, so she could address the diminutive Said head-on. "Thank you, my friend. There's no way we'd have made it this far without you."

Said glanced shyly at the ground. "I am proud to serve."

Elijah walked past both of them, and they turned to watch, as he approached the tablets. Zya rose and, taking Said by the hand, followed close behind. With Anubis' chilling effect gone, the tablets glowed brighter than ever, filling the cavern with a warm, green light.

"Look!" Elijah exclaimed.

The light had revealed a hidden opening behind the crumbled rubble Anubis emerged from. An exit. But Zya's focus was on the tablets.

"First things first," she said.

Letting go of Said's hand she, once again, approached the granite altar. Just as before, the tablets called to her, as if she was connected to them by some invisible string. They beckoned her forth and Zya almost reached out again, until she felt Elijah's hand on her arm.

"Are you sure you want to do that?" he asked, with a mischievous glint in his eye. "You *do* remember what happened last time."

Zya stuck out her tongue, but she knew he was right. "Well, why don't you tell us what you'd do, Mr. Glowing Tablet Expert."

He stuck his tongue out back, and then turned to study the tablets. As he leaned in, his timepiece began to activate and out of it materialized what looked like a magnifying glass. At first, he was surprised, but proceeded to continue the exam.

"Said," he called, beckoning their native friend over. "Can you tell me what this means?"

The little boy stood on his tip-toes and craned his neck. "That's the Old Tongue."

"The 'Old Tongue'?" Elijah asked.

"It was spoken by The Founders, but it hasn't been heard for thousands of years," he said. "Even before the Archons arrived."

"Hmmm," Elijah contemplated. He looked down at the timepiece on his wrist, and studied it for a moment. Grasping the dial that circumnavigated the watch face, he twisted. And, as he did so, the lens of the magnifying glass changed. He turned it again, and the lenses swapped in and out, like a reading test at the eye doctor. Eventually, Elijah stopped.

"Wowwwww," he whispered.

"What?" Zya asked.

"I can *see* it ... I mean, I can *read* it ... I can actually read the inscriptions."

"What does it say?" she pressed.

"Imbue your spirit with the thirst for wisdom, brand your mind with the power of knowledge, write in your heart that which you wish to keep, and you will never be without," he went on. "Listen before you speak, ask with a heart of gold, and all shall be given."

Silence echoed throughout the cavern, as the words hung in the air.

"What in the goodness gracious does that mean?" Elijah exclaimed.

"Shhh," Zya hissed.

Once again, everything was quiet. But all was not still. Fresh air was streaming into the chamber through the newly excavated opening, and Zya was sure she could hear a whisper in the wind.

"Sssssubmitttttttt," the air whisked through the empty passageways. "Sssssurrenderrr."

Zy had always been a fighter. All you had to do was ask Elijah and he'd tell you — she wasn't one to back down. Wasn't one to give up, either. For some reason, she didn't know why, Zya felt a responsibility to finish what she started. And, every time somebody doubted her, or said she couldn't do it, it fueled the fire inside. She was a rebel, through and through. Zya hated authority and couldn't stand know-it-all adults (who didn't really know anything) telling her what to do. What was it to them, anyway? But this wasn't her mother barking orders, or one of her classmates trying to gain the upper hand. This was a different world, with different rules, and victory would require an act of trust.

She stood still, and spoke aloud, as if the cave could hear her. "I, Zya Nicole Jenkins, Guardian of the Cosmic Clocks, pledge to keep the power of the Emerald Tablets. To wield it only in defense of the defenseless, and against the forces of evil."

As her words rippled out like a healing balm, they breathed new life into the Emerald Tablets, the steady hum at their core becoming a loud roar. A column of wind formed around the granite altar, and Zya, Elijah and Said looked on as the glowing ball of wind and fire lifted the tablets off the stand. Said dropped to his knees and touched his face to the ground as the maelstrom filled the entire cave. Then, the next moment, in a brilliant flash, the emerald storm shrunk to the size of a grain of rice and was sucked, quite dramatically, into Zya's timepiece.

She looked down, breathless. All was still again and, on the face of the watch, a tiny green icon, which resembled two small tablets, lit up with a swell of emerald energy. A wave surged throughout the instrument, crackling through every circuit and gear, before returning to a dim pulsating glow.

"Woah." Elijah remarked.

Zya walked over to Said, who had become completely prostrate, and picked him up off the floor. But, even when he was standing again, the young Earthling kept his eyes trained on the floor, unwilling to look her in the face. Zya gently placed two fingers underneath his chin and raised it until their eyes met. He pushed her hand off and lowered his head again.

"I'm not worthy," he said.

She pulled his chin up again, and smiled a warm smile. "You, my friend, are *most* worthy."

"Buttt … but … the gods have chosen *you*," he stammered. "And I'm just a peasant boy. A slave, at that."

"You are no such thing," she said, taking his hand between hers. "You're no more a slave than I'm an alien."

Said smiled. "Welllll …"

Zya smiled back. "I may be from far away, but I belong here, too, just as much as you do."

"You're our friend," Elijah added. "In fact, I don't know many people who would've done for us what you have, risking your life and all."

Said's eyes welled up and, this time, the dam broke, pouring streams of water down his cheeks. Placing one hand on his shoulder, Zya used the cuff of her jacket to wipe away the saltwater.

"I want to be free," Said whispered. "More than anything, I want to be free."

"You already are, my friend."

CHAPTER SIXTEEN

Let My People Go

The gentle waves of the Nile River licked at the base of the Temple of Thoth. The sun was just beginning to peek over the horizon, bathing the temple face in a glorious cavalcade of light. A single massive stone doorframe stood alone, like a little keyhole, up against the monstrous wall. The temple had been constructed to precise specifications so that, every day at daybreak, the light of the rising sun would kiss the tip of its brilliance on the temple shrine. And, this was that time. The bright morning star streamed through the doorway, the corners of its rays gradually converging on each other until it resembled the tip of a sharp knife.

It was that beam which, for a passing moment, warmed the surface of an expertly crafted granite shrine. In the center of an eight-by-six slab, a rectangular tower, about waist high and thick as a human, jutted out of the granite with a large, round brass basin affixed to the top. Directly above the basin, an unwrapped infant, also made of the hard, jet-black rock — and not very happy about the situation, from the expression on its face — lay in the outstretched arms of Thoth himself. He held the supine infant high above his head in the palms of his hands, as if offering it up, to god knows whom. Thoth's head, which resembled that of a bird and sported the long curved beak of the Ibis, was also the color of granite. Just like Anubis, Thoth had the body of a man, and yet, seemed to be anything but. Directly above the navel, a small circular hole, no more than a millimeter across, and almost imperceptible to the naked eye, drew the sun's attention, as it sliced down Thoth's torso. Through this unholy portal, the morning light penetrated a three-meter-thick wall, to which the statue was affixed, and poured, like a laser beam into an ancient corridor, where Said's little rodent nose sniffed furiously. He signaled to the Guardians with a series of squeaks, and scurried down the wall to safety.

"Stand back," Zya warned.

She held a fist across her chest, so that the face of the timepiece was pointed at the wall ahead. Then, Zya inhaled. Focusing everything she had on the tiny hole, she attempted to unleash the might of the Emerald Tablets. At first, nothing happened and an awkward silence filled the space.

"If this doesn't work, I don't think I'm skinny enough to get through," Elijah said.

Zya remembered the lesson in the cave. *Breathe. Listen. Surrender.* She calmed herself, letting go of everything but the task at hand, and, as Elijah looked on, the watch began to spark with wisps of emerald magic. Finally, a bright green beam of pure energy came forth from the face of the watch. It tore through the thick, hard wall as if cutting through parchment paper, shattering the shrine and scattering the statue in pieces. Thoth's head rolled, ignominiously, to a rest, as the posse of freedom fighters climbed through the opening and into the temple chamber.

Zya touched her timepiece and spoke into it. "Maroun? Nimrod, do you copy? Nimrod, this is the Guardians. Please copy."

But there was no response.

The blast had decimated the shrine, busting the wall wide open and strewing the remains into a dusty half-circle. Said walked up to Thoth's severed head and stared at it silently. The infant lay broken, clean in half, a few feet away. As the sun continued to ascend, its rays bathed the temple in a deep, ominous red.

"What is this place?" Zya asked Said.

"The Temple of Thoth," he said.

"Thoth?" Elijah asked.

"He was the first of the Archons to rule Earth, more than a thousand years ago," Said recalled. "Regarded as the god of magic, wisdom and the moon, he brought writing, astronomy, mathematics and created the calendar while ruling for nearly five hundred years. Then, one day, he disappeared."

They walked out of the inner sanctum and into a single, massive room the size of a warehouse. A sacred silence hung in the air as the children surveyed the space, staring up into the vaulted ceiling. It was cool in the temple and the morning sun was warm on their skin. Between the door and where they now stood, there were two more statues, one on the right and one on the left. They were anonymous, androgynous, identical and stood directly across from one another, like a reflection in a mirror. Each effigy presided over a flat stone table, holding, in one hand, a bowl and, the other, a knife, aimed ominously at the table below. On the ground, at the foot of each stone slab, was a large clay jar.

"I don't think this place is for magic shows or full moon meditations," Elijah mumbled.

"No, it's not," Said replied. "Thoth is also known as the God of Balance, so the Harvest Festival is held in his honor."

"Well, *that* makes more sense," Elijah said. "This place *reeks*."

Said looked at him, confused. "I don't smell anything."

"Of evil, my friend. Of evil."

Then, the little boy had a moment of recognition. "She was here," he said. "I can feel it."

Zya extended a hand and placed it gently on his shoulder. "We'll bring them to justice for what they've done. To her, and everyone else."

"I don't want justice." Said admitted. "I want them to hurt, the way they hurt her."

"I get it," Zya said. "But that's not justice, my friend. The hurt only stops when *we* stop it."

"Why do they get to hurt us, and we don't get to hurt them back?"

"No one *gets* to hurt anyone," she said. "Sometimes people are selfish, or mean, or they just think they're better than you. People use all kinds of reasons to justify the things they do — it's our restraint that makes us different."

"What if they're trying to hurt you?" he asked. "Are you just supposed to stand there and take it?"

"Don't ever be afraid to defend what you love," Zya said. "Just make sure not to lose yourself in the process."

Said nodded, as if he understood, and he had no more to say at the moment. So, the band continued on, past the stone tables and toward the rising sun, which was, now, almost halfway over the horizon. It was stunning to behold the big, bright half-circle shining red, yellow, orange and magenta. As they passed through the door frame, they couldn't help but marvel at its size. The opening, which might have appeared small if you saw it from the opposite bank, was at least four men tall and two-and-a-half men across. It was unusually large, even for the reptilians, which only added to the exotic allure of this solemn, and foreboding, place. Through the doorway was a grand deck, spacious enough to hold a battalion of troops, or land a fighter jet. It was made out of the same massive granite blocks, as the rest of the place and the stones were smooth to the touch, even at the crease between them. In fact, especially there. Each monolith fit together perfectly with the others, as if they were one, rather than many. It was a work of art, by a master craftsman no doubt.

The river was calm and the sky was clear, so one could see straight across to the other shore. Reeds and long, thick grass lined the shallows, in both directions, far as the eye could see. But, right in front of the deck, which jutted out past the reeds, there was nothing but pure, unadulterated blue. The Nile was life, after all, and life was abundant. There were herons and crocodiles, and fish of all company and kind.

"This is where they bring the boats," Said remarked. "Then they go up that way."

Zya turned to follow Said's finger and was struck by the grandiose beauty of the sight before her. It was like a dream or something. She even pinched herself. Less than a football field away, just a touch to Zya's right, lay the Sphinx. The watchful cat, with the head of a man and headdress of a pharaoh, patiently guarded the banks of the Nile. It faced directly toward the rising sun, which caused it to seem as if it was in a neverending staring contest.

"If I'm correct," Elijah said, pointing first at the middle pyramid. "That's the Pyramid of Khafre, which would make the one to its right the Great Pyramid of Khufu."

Said made a sour face. "Not quite."

He pointed to the one Elijah had called Khafre. "This is the Pyramid of Thoth, and the big one was built by Enki, himself, hundreds of years ago."

Zy looked to the left and there was the least of the great triangular monuments, complete with its own temple complex. The temple, just like all the others, was connected to the pyramid by a long causeway made up of two water-filled trenches, with a walkway in between. The water flowed straight up to the base of the pyramid and, then, disappeared inside. Zya closed her eyes and listened closely. She could feel a subtle vibration rippling through the air, and remembered their conversation with Maroun.

"The depression field," Zya said. "I can feel it."

"Depression field?" Said asked.

"Based on what the Lumerians told us, it's most likely a dampening field of some sort," Elijah interjected.

"Could *that* be what's making it hard for us to change?" asked the little native boy.

Elijah cocked an eyebrow. "It could be."

Then, Zya turned to Eli. "How can we stop it?"

He stroked his chin and looked off into the distance. As the sunrise hit the crown of Enki's pyramid, the golden cap glistened magnificently, throwing sparkling rays of shimmering light into the atmosphere. They were spectacular. They were marvelous. They were … well, if that wasn't it! Elijah snapped his fingers, as an excited smile spread across his face.

"The caps," he said. "Gold is a conductor."

"Are you saying," Zya ventured, "that, if we take out the caps we can kill the energy field?"

"It's a reasonable assumption," Eli responded. "No caps, no way to transmit the energy. Well, it's a bit more complicated than that, but … you get the picture."

"We need to shut them down," Said, jumped in. "We need to shut them down now."

"Of course," Zya assured him. "That's why we're here."

"Easier said than done, though," Elijah jumped in. "We'll have to expose ourselves to get in range."

Zya pondered for a moment and then turned to Said. "Go," she said, firmly. "Bring back anyone who will fight. Tell your people, the time is now."

His eyes sparkled, and the dirty little face cracked a wide smile. "We would be honored to fight by your side."

"Go, then," she said. "Quickly, my friend."

With one last bow, Said returned to the form in which he had come to them and skittered off towards the settlements.

"Okay," Elijah asked with a twinkle in his eye, "Now what, Fearless Leader?"

Zya smiled, but it was an uncomfortable smile. She could feel the weight of his words, and he was right. Ultimately, it was up to her now. Whether they were able to pull through would most certainly depend on what she did next. *I don't know if I have what it takes*, she said to herself. The pressure was on, and they needed her — Elijah, the Earthlings, the Lumerians — they all needed her, and she couldn't let them down. It was just then that, once again, she heard her grandma's calm voice. *You don't need to be anybody but you, baby. Just do what you do, and it'll all work out in the end.*

"I think we can use the tablets to take them out," she said to Elijah. "You just have to help me get close enough."

"That's not much of a plan," Elijah wrinkled his forehead, "But, it just might work."

CHAPTER SEVENTEEN

Knock, Knock, Knockin' at Heaven's Door

The Guardians skated down the causeway toward their destiny, jumping over water and land. Three quick steps, and a jump; two-and-a-half more, and then another. Over and over, they sped away from the sun, which was now nearly over the horizon. Their smiles were wider than ever, and Elijah thought to himself that they'd never moved so freely.

Just as the thought escaped, a sound like thunder ripped through the air and Enki descended from the heavens. He hovered down, positioning himself directly in front of his predecessor's pyramid. The children stopped in their tracks, sliding to a stand-still. Glancing at each other, they shared a look of astonishment. The god-king seemed bigger than before and, indeed, he was. It was as if Enki had taken on his most fearsome form yet, nearly quadrupling in size. Two giant wings, like that of an angel or a Pegasus, were spread out behind him, relaxing, as he hung, effortlessly, in the air. He was covered head-to-toe in battle armor, which sparkled white in the light of the sun. Behind him, a dozen flying saucers, also a bright metallic, slid into position on his flank.

"Well, hello," his voice boomed.

He raised his hands and the Nile came to him, like two, big swirling pillars. Zya and Elijah watched in awe as the waters obeyed his call, enveloping the Lizard King in a swirling ball of aquatic force.

"You've been far too much trouble," he said. "I should have finished you before."

"Maybe if you didn't like the sound of your own voice so much," Elijah muttered.

"Is that right, boy?" Enki said, curling the corners of his mouth in a mocking grin. "Then, why are you shaking?"

Elijah looked down and, indeed, just as the god-pharaoh had said, his hands were spasming uncontrollably.

"We're not afraid of you," Zya yelled across the sands, as she stepped forward, positioning herself between her friend and the Lizard King.

"You've enslaved this planet for far too long," she said. "You've killed their fathers, taken their children and denied them their birthright as free people. You're right, this ends now. But it will be your end, not ours."

"Oh?" said Enki, still amused. "And who's going to stop me? Two *children*?"

Zya fumed. "We're not *children* ..."

And, then, as if both were on the very same wavelength, the two Guardians stepped forward, clasping a closed fist across their chests. Their timepieces sparkled in the sun, and Elijah's voice joined the chorus, "We're the Guardians of the Cosmic Clocks."

Without warning, Zya fired a bolt of glowing green energy straight at the Archon king. He dodged just in time but the beam hit a flying saucer behind him, leaving nothing but embers and smoke. Enki's face filled with rage as he turned the full might of the Nile against them, shooting a stream — as if from a giant firehose — directly at the two heroes. But the Guardians were quick on their feet, deftly avoiding the attack. Even so, Enki would not stop. Relentlessly, he channeled the waters toward them, and was only ever a split-second behind, though it might as well have been forever.

"Split up!" Zya yelled.

Elijah nodded and split off, zigzagging straight for the Lizard King. For a moment, the god-pharaoh was taken off guard, and it was just the moment they needed. Ascending straight into the sky, Enki doubled his distance from the ground in a matter of seconds. As he gained perspective, he noticed Zya was flying in the opposite direction, on a beeline for the smallest pyramid.

"Captain Curran, intercept the girl," Enki commanded.

On his orders, three of the saucers split off from the main group. They were on top of her in a matter of moments but, this time, Zya was ready. Just as they moved to intercept her, she executed a three-jump pattern, expertly tracing a giant "Z". As she emerged from each jump, Zya released a perfectly placed beam of green energy at each ship and, in the blink of an eye, all three had been reduced to clouds. Two more jumps and she was in range. Zya aimed true, unleashing a continuous wave of energy directly on the golden cap. The conductive metal absorbed the energy, but it had nowhere to go. Nowhere but down. Down, down, down, into the inner workings of the pyramid, through the King's Chamber, and the Queen's Chamber, and countless halls and passageways, the green glow surged. And, then, as it pooled at the base, the emerald energy circled back into itself and, igniting in a green flame, pushed the blast back up, up, up, and out the tip of the pyramid, blowing the golden coronet clean off.

Zya surveyed the destruction and gave a sigh of relief. *That worked better than I'd hoped*, she said to herself. And, as she jumped back to join her friend, she could already feel some of the pressure subside. But the explosion had distracted Elijah, which Enki used to catch the Guardian unaware. Recognizing a pattern in his movements, Enki timed a blast of water to meet Elijah just as he re-materialized. The lanky teen tumbled backward, head-over-foot, and landed with a face full of wet sand. Zy was there before you could even blink, helping Eli up while brushing him off in the process.

"That was quite a performance," she teased. "Is that a new dismount you're working on?"

"Funny." Elijah spit out a mouthful of sand.

She chuckled.

"It worked though," he said, smiling.

"Yup. Chain reaction, just like you said. Now we only need to get to the other two."

Elijah finally looked up, and his eyes became big as grapes.

"What?" Zya asked.

All he did was raise his arm and point. She turned to see Enki, floating cross-legged in some kind of meditative trance. At first, it wasn't clear what he was up to but, as Enki meditated, two wisps of dark, swirling energy made for the mouth of the nearest pyramid. There, at the mouth of the base, two massive stone pharaohs stood guard. They had to be thirty meters tall, at least. And, as the dark magic entered them, they began to move. Just like in the cave, they separated from the wall as an avalanche of rubble crumbled to the ground. *He's controlling them with his mind*, Zya realized.

"Ghouls, zombies, lizard aliens and, now ... *this?*" Elijah muttered to himself.

Zya grabbed him by the shoulders and gave him a gentle smack on the cheek. "Just a little longer," she said. "Just stick with me a little longer."

"Always," he whispered, returning her gaze. "Just promise me one thing."

"What?"

"You're gonna have to figure out how to take these things down. I'm *slightly* overwhelmed at the moment."

"Deal." She smiled, as they clasped their palms together.

And, then, something unexpected happened. When their palms touched, a blue spark of magic energy swirled around their joined hands, and the gears of their watches began to whirr. They were spinning up, spitting out sparks of blue and white energy. But this was something different. It felt ancient, and powerful, and Zya let go, stepping back, breathless.

"What was that?" Elijah asked, wrinkling his nose and cocking his head to the side.

"I don't know," she said. "But I think I know how to use it."

CHAPTER EIGHTEEN

Yea, Though I Walk Through the Valley of the Shadow of Death

Just as Zya finished explaining her plan, two dozen Archons in mechanized battle suits dropped out of the UFOs like a swarm of yellowjackets. At first, they seemed to plummet to the ground. And, then, jetpacks firing a thousand miles a minute, they managed to reorient themselves, eventually making a bee-line straight for the Guardians.

"See you on the other side," she said with a wink.

Elijah saluted, and they both gave a little laugh.

The troopers were nearly on top of them now, and the Guardians steeled themselves for battle. There was no need to rush in, so they waited patiently, allowing the Archon guards to come to them. The soldiers broke out of flight about fifty feet away, orienting themselves to fire their plasma cannons. Then, disappearing from her spot beside Elijah, Zya materialized twenty feet above ground, directly in front of the lead lizard. Red canvas All-Stars flashing across the sky, she landed a roundhouse kick to the jaw, causing saliva to spray as the captain's tongue flopped out of his mouth.

"It's on," Elijah said, jumping into the fray.

The Guardians were too quick for the unwieldy reptiles. By now, they were well-acquainted with their timepieces and used the time in-between jumps masterfully. A solid strategy of unpredictability was the key, they'd learned — don't let your enemy get a read on you. It was like a real-life game of chess, and they had a knack for the game, just in slightly different ways. Zya was bold and athletic. She overwhelmed the soldiers by taking the risky path. Rather than cautiously keeping her distance, she got as close as humanly possible, which worked more than a few times before they started catching on. Elijah, on the other hand, was one for artful unpredictability, and a little bit of smoke-and-mirror. He wasn't as athletic, or strong, as Zya, so he relied more on his mind, and took pleasure in finding a novel way to take down each new adversary. It was like a fascinating riddle. Anticipate where they would be before they knew they would be there.

They made their way thusly, constantly suspended in the East African sky. In fact, to the untrained observer, it might have appeared as if they were flying. Eventually, the lizards caught on to Zya's strategy and she had to switch it up, going for the legs, or appearing behind them, instead. On the other side, however, Elijah jumped past the battalion completely and aimed himself straight at the Great Pyramid. A handful of soldiers broke off to give chase, but he was already in the clear, with nothing in his way but open skies. He knew he couldn't do any real damage without the Emerald Tablets, but the Archons didn't. For all they knew, it could've been the timepiece itself that had the kind of power Zya displayed. So, half of the remaining ships broke formation, positioning themselves between the Guardian and the Great Pyramid. The giant stone pharaohs lumbered forward, shaking the ground with every step, and it appeared as if they were both caught.

Just then, Zya jumped out of the scrum and Elijah swung around on a dime, doubling back so they were on a collision course. The troopers tried to chase them, but they were no more successful than the Fiends, or the palace guards. The Guardians converged on the gargantuan Goliaths, who both tried, and failed, to swat them down.

They were simply too quick. Zya jumped to the shoulder of the closest one and Elijah bounded off the other's head as they both vaulted, simultaneously, into the space between. It was an act of belief, a trust fall — to reach out, take a leap and know that your friend will be there, just like they promised.

The Guardians floated toward one another, arms outstretched before them. But, just before they met, the Guardians began to fall. Like two stones dropped from a great height, they hurtled through the air, grasping for the other in a frenzy. And, again. And, again. Until, finally, their hands met. This time, when the sparks began, Zya focused all her energy on the connection, meditating on the feeling of Elijah's hand in hers, of his skin on her skin. And, so Elijah did, as well, as he had been instructed. They hung on for dear life as their timepieces spun up with that same white-blue glow, which grew from the size of a tiny seed to a human-sized cocoon, which enveloped them both completely. The Guardians hung, suspended in space, protective energy swirling around them in streaks and streams, like planets around the sun, or rings around a planet. And, they were at the center, hands locked, with looks of terror and surprise plastered on their faces. It was as if time had actually stopped.

The stone monstrosities had been reaching out to grab them, but, now, they, too, were frozen in time, unable to get any closer, no matter how much they might try. See, life is a game of seconds and inches, with sometimes the smallest margin determining victory or defeat. All of a sudden, Zya smiled and it was as if space itself constricted, shrinking back into itself, over and over again. And, then, without warning, it expanded again, creating a shock wave strong enough to turn stone to dust. The blast flattened everything within a hundred meters, knocking Enki to the ground and returning his mind to its rightful place. The thunderous rush short-circuited ships and jetpacks alike, reducing the front half of Thoth's pyramid to rubble. With so much of its base gone, the golden cap was unable to balance any longer, teetering, tipping, and, finally, sliding off the structure like a child at the playground.

For a moment, everything was quiet. The Guardians drifted lightly to the ground, as if floating on top of a cloud, and held each other tightly, smiling all the while.

"It worked!" Zya exclaimed.

"More like 'succeeded spectacularly,'" Elijah said, surveying the aftermath.

But there wasn't a moment to rest. A sudden crack of thunder and lightning brought them back to Earth. Over the curve of the desert, Enki rose up, once more, his eyes rippling with angry bolts of electric energy. Now, not only did the waters of the Nile obey him, but clouds formed overhead, as well. The Guardians looked up just as the first giant drops — each nearly as big as a human head — began to splatter on the sand.

"We've got him on the ropes," Zya said. "Let's finish this."

"Aye, aye, captain."

They turned to see Enki hovering in front of the Great Pyramid, a swirling pillar of electrified water surrounding the god-king like a mile-high electric fence. Then, he ordered the clouds to open and doused the desert plain with wave, after wave, after wave. At first, the Guardians did their best to avoid the aquatic bombs, jumping back and forth. But, after about thirty seconds or so, even the magic of their watches could not withstand the force of nature. Elijah emerged from a jump and was pummeled by a particularly large drop, knocking him onto his back. Enki seized on the misstep, shooting a super-charged beam of electric water and knocking him unconscious.

"No!" Zya screamed through the downpour.

Then, the Lizard King produced a large green amulet from around his neck and aimed it at the helpless Guardian. A continuous green light streamed from the amulet and came to rest on Elijah's prone body. But, rather than destroy him, Zya watched as the beam transformed him into a scaly lizard himself. Unlike the Archons, who walked upright, he looked more like a Komodo Dragon, sporting a long snout, four short legs and a powerful tail. But he was a reptilian, nonetheless. Enki had played the most cruel trick imaginable, and turned her friend into one of *them*. But he would never be the enemy to her. Without a thought, she jumped to her friend's side, cradling his head as he lay there struggling to breathe. His skin smelled of singed hair, which, when mixed with the deluge, created an aroma something like wet, burning tar. And, for the first time since their adventure had started, Zya wished they were home, and wept in the downpour.

Then, in little more than an instant, the rain broke, skies cleared, and Enki laughed a deep, bellowing laugh, baring his sharp teeth through a devious grin. "You aren't so defiant now, are you, little girl?" He said. "I told you you'd learn your place."

She stood up and, glaring at the giant lizard, screamed over the desert plain. "What'd you do to my friend?"

"Only what he had coming, my dear," Enki smiled cruelly. "But you ... you will suffer."

"Do your *worst*," she glared even harder.

Wasting no time, Zya seized the element of surprise and, in two jumps, was on top of the Lizard King. Enki met her with a fury, as the remaining ships looked on. The two champions moved so fast that those watching could only see a blur. Like two hummingbirds, dancing with death, they moved, trading blows back and forth. At first, Zya seemed to have the upper hand and Enki was on the defense, as she was dealing blows left and right. But, despite connecting, her efforts had little to no effect, and she began to tire.

Just then, as Zya was nearing the end of her strength, a chorus of squeaks echoed over the dunes. Moments later, Said's head popped over a giant mound of sand. He was coming toward them, and he wasn't alone. Bays, growls, squawks and squeaks preceded a contingent of horses, wildebeest, hawks, herons and a hippo, as they streamed down the dunes. The Archon soldiers snapped to attention and rushed to meet them, the two groups converging on one another like an inevitability. The uproar could be heard across the desert wastes, reaching the village streets and echoing in the ears of the people.

For a moment, everything hung in the balance. The Lizard King versus the Guardian — liberator and oppressor — locked in a cosmic duel of the fates. They went blow for blow. Zya was relentless and determined but Enki was big and strong. His soldiers descended on the animal platoon and, for a second, it seemed that all was lost. As the reptilian guard surged against the ragtag resistance, Enki cocked back his massive fist. But the freedom fighters would not be beaten so easily. They were fighting for their lives, after all. Just as the door seemed like it might close, the brute squad lunged at the Archon guards with a wildness in their eyes, and Zya aimed her timepiece at the heart of the Lizard King.

CHAPTER NINETEEN

With a Little Help from My Friends

Time seemed to stand still and Zya could see everything clearly — her friend, lying helplessly on the ground, the Brotherhood locked in mortal combat and Enki's electrified fist, mere millimeters from her nose. Just as the grasping hands of the stone statues had gotten close, but not close enough, the god-king was too late. Zya unleashed the full might of the Emerald Tablets, catapulting him backward so forcefully he traveled like a bullet out of a gun. Enki hit the ground like a skipping stone over calm water, and tumbled, over and over, like a neverending backward somersault, before skipping one last time and sticking in the side of a large dune.

The guards and animals tore at one another. Desperate screeches and blood-curdling screams punctuated the action, as the sound of teeth and beaks against blades and electro-staves rang out across the expanse. Slash, growl, chomp. Pew, pew, pew. Eventually, the soldiers realized it was in their best interests to lean on their long-range weapons — in fact, a few had already suffered fatal wounds at the hands of the freedom fighters. So, they took to the skies and started to pick off the Earthlings one-by-one. The Brotherhood countered with their hawks and herons, sending them to pick and claw at the lizard people, which they did to some success, knocking a few of them back to Earth.

By now, the sounds of battle had reached all corners of the land, and the people came out to see what all the commotion was about. They gathered, close enough to see but far enough away as not to be in danger. Everyone had brought a little something with, and, whatever they had, no matter how little or how much, most were happy to share until it was gone. So, they freely doled out their fruits and nuts, and water and tea. One man even brought a sack of small, rectangular puzzle cubes for the children to play with. And not one of them thought twice about it. To these people, giving was not a loss, but rather a gift itself. It was a blessing and honor to share what they had with the group. After all, those who had joined here together would be one of them, now and forever.

Zya was laser-focused, her eyes following the god-pharaoh unrelentingly, as his body bounced across the desert sand. When he came to a stop, she jumped immediately to his location and, as he attempted to pick himself up, landed a swift, crippling kick to the chin. Well, it would've been crippling to almost anyone else. But this was the Lord of Earth, Pharaoh of the Dynastic Throne and High Priest to the gods. So, as she aimed at him again, he reached out his massive right hand and grabbed her by the throat, flicking the watch off her wrist with a single flourish of his long, curved claw. The timepiece flew through the air and fell, harmlessly, to the ground a full fifty feet away. Despite trying to free herself from the long-fingered hand, Zya could see no way out. His grip was tight, and she had no more cards up her sleeve.

She was cooked. There would be no way out of this one, and no one was coming to save her. *This is it*, she thought. *This must be how it ends*. She looked up into the bright blue sky, as Enki squeezed harder. She could draw no more breath and, at the center of her vision, a small black dot appeared. It began to grow, larger and larger, until she was sure she could go any minute now. A flash of light caught her eye, and she figured this was it. But, then, she heard and felt the blast of a big weapon. Before she knew what was happening, both she and the Lizard King were flying through the air, and he released her from his grip. Despite the pain aching in her bones, she welcomed the feeling of tumbling, head-over-heel, through the sand. At least she wasn't in that slimy lizard's hand anymore. And, besides, it kind of felt like a bunch of clouds.

Once she came to a stop, Zya willed herself up. She was pretty sure one of the blasts had hit the god-king directly, and he lay on his back, unconscious. She continued to scan the area and was surprised to catch a glint of metal not more than a hop, skip and jump from where she stood. She ran over to the shiny object and, indeed, by some apparent stroke of luck, it was her timepiece. She shook off the sand and slipped the device back on, just as a hologram crackled to life. It was Maroun — well, a projection of him anyway — standing on the small, circular face.

"Are you alright, my child?"

She looked up and saw the bright, metallic hull of the Nimrod slicing through the air. They engaged the remaining Archon ships, chasing them back behind the Great Pyramid.

She growled into the communicator. "*Child?!*"

"Our champion," Maroun responded. "Now, go finish this."

Zya smiled. "Oh ... and Maroun?"

"Yes, Ms. Jenkins."

"Thanks."

The line went silent, and Zya felt a calm, like nothing she'd ever experienced. The feeling washed over her body, and it felt as if the fear had left her completely. She was still here, but there was no more mystery, and possibility was everywhere. She'd stared death in the face and lived to tell about it, which was no small feat. Zya gazed at the rising sun, as it shined upon her face, and realized that her journey had just begun. Somehow, she knew that all would be well. Breathing in, she thought of her friend and, before another moment had passed, Zya was at his side, cradling his face in her hands.

"You're coming back with me," she whispered. "You know that, right?"

She thought she could see his face twitch, and a single tear rolled down her cheek. "You're coming back with me."

Closing her eyes again, Zya heard a voice. It spoke to her, in the way of the Lumerians, and seemed to be some sort of poem. Over and over again, she heard the voice in her head. It was a little voice, and yet persistent. She could see it in her mind and hear it in her ears, and she understood it. How, she wasn't quite certain. But what she was sure of is that something miraculous had just happened. She couldn't explain it, but that didn't make it any less of a miracle. In fact, perhaps more so.

And, then, kneeling there, she spoke the words out loud.

الماضي والمستقبل، الآن، اتحدوا / في أحلك ساعات الليل / النار والماء والأرض والسماء / انهضوا، استيقظوا

almadi walmustaqbal, al'aan, ittahiduu / fi'ahlak saa'at al-layl / an-naar wal-maa' wal-'ard was-samaa' / inhadu, istayqizhuu

"Past and future, now, unite / In the darkest hour of night / Fire, water, earth and sky / Arise, awaken."

As the final sounds escaped her lips, a small wisp of green light spirited out of her timepiece, like a string made of silk, and leapt its way into the nostrils of the beast, looping back out through its mouth, and returning, ultimately, into the watch. Zya could feel the power of Enki's amulet flow into her wrist and, as the Emerald Tablets absorbed the corruptible energy, the body in her arms slowly began to change. Before long, it, once more, resembled the young man she knew. His eyes were closed and, below the wide set nose and furrowed brow, Elijah's lips were pursed in a slight frown, as if he were trying to answer a difficult question. She lowered her ear to his face and, listening real close, was able to hear the sound of shallow breathing.

"You just sit tight," she whispered. "It'll be over before you know it."

Zya kissed him on the forehead and lay his head down gently on the sand. Then, rising triumphantly, she surveyed the desert plain. She could see the Nimrod, cloaking, and uncloaking, over the Great Pyramid, as it jumped back and forth to avoid the Archon attacks. Then, her eyes found him. This had to end, and it had to end now. Enki was all knotted up, half buried, in the side of a sand dune right at the base of the Great Pyramid. She jumped to the spot and poked him with her toe. Just as she touched him, he swept his giant hand at her. But, this time, Zya was ready and jumped back to avoid the attack. As Enki climbed to his feet, he seemed more menacing than ever, a tower of supernatural powers. Zya stood proudly, on the pyramid side of the god-king and, despite his shadow engulfing her, refused to back down.

"I'm not afraid of you," she yelled.

"I know," he said. "And that's why I must crush you."

"You can try," she said.

"Like a fly between my fingers."

Once again, Zya seized the element of surprise. Jumping the two-and-a-half stories onto Enki's shoulder, she boxed his ear, backflipping off just before he could get at her. In this same way, she wore down the Lord of Earth, hitting, and running, and hitting again. Every time he reached for her she would jump to safety, only to attack once his guard had dropped again. This desperate, determined twelve-year-old girl outwitted and out-maneuvered the Lizard King over, and over, and over again, until he was exactly where she wanted him. Enki stood, hands on his knees, panting loudly.

"You are a worthy adversary, child, but you will never win."

"Whatever I am," she said. "I think I was made to bring you down."

And, for maybe the first time ever, the lizard alien god-pharaoh squirmed uncomfortably. The Archon pontiff, who'd ruled the planet for hundreds of years and won countless battles against vaunted warriors, felt fear. The conviction in her voice, and her utter determination, made him uneasy. He could feel, deep down, there was something different about this girl. But he dared not show weakness.

"You can't destroy me," Enki goaded her. "You don't have what it takes."

Zya laughed. "You've enslaved this planet for far too long."

"You'll have to pry it from my cold, dead claws," he shot back. "But I don't think you have it in you."

"You're right, I don't want to kill you," she said. "But this has to end. So, why don't we let the tablets decide? Let *them* judge us."

With a flick of her wrist, Zya brought the tablets to life and, simultaneously, she and the Lizard King were seized by a bolt of pure green light. The energy surged from head-to-toe and finger-to-finger, so it looked as if they were stretched out on a cross. The electric green poured from their eyes, mouths, fingers, toes and the very tops of their heads. Not one molecule was left unturned, as the pure green light traversed every inch of their innermost selves, washing away the contradictions until there was only one. They glowed bright, even in the light of the sun, and bathed the desert plain in a green light, as the onlookers gaped in awe. And, then, in the blink of an eye, the beam that ran through Enki seemed to accelerate in speed. He screamed a scream of eternal agony, as the emerald energy expanded outward, leaving nothing but the empty space where he had been.

At that very moment, Zya regained consciousness and was returned to herself. Still hovering midair, the Guardian breathed in, channeling the light within toward the Great Pyramid. It beamed bright as ever, making contact with the broad side of the monument and instantly incinerating two of the Archon ships. The shot hit home with such force that it could've been heard across the sea, a stream of interdimensional energy carving a hole the size of an eighteen-wheeler. It burned clear through the center, almost as if the hole had been seared by a hot poker, leaving the walls around it instantly cauterized, so that one could see straight to the other side. Though the final cap remained, there was nothing left of the insides and, so, thus, the final vestiges of control were wiped away.

In fact, the air already seemed lighter.

The last remaining Archon guards retreated to their ships and disappeared into the atmosphere. Only about half of the Brotherhood remained, but the survivors were ecstatic, releasing a primal cry. They'd fought valiantly, and had triumphed. And, for the first time in their lives, they were free.

Zya jumped to where they stood, as animals all around her shifted back to their human forms. Those who'd been watching from afar, streamed over the desert plain to check on their friends, and join the celebration. As she surveyed the scene, a large lion, tall as Zya's shoulders, bounded up to where she stood and started licking her face. At first, she was startled. But she reminded herself that, now, they were only amongst friends. And, just then, the beast before her transformed into a skinny little boy. It was her friend, Said, and they hugged and smiled.

"How'd you do that?" Zya asked.

"I could ask you the same," he responded.

She winked.

"Where's your friend?" he asked.

"Oh!" she said out loud. "Elijah!"

Zya returned to where she'd left him, and there he lay, peaceful as ever. His expression had returned to a calm, relaxed smile, and he seemed so serene Zya hesitated to wake him. She leaned over his body and listened again for breathing. But she didn't hear anything, this time. *Oh, no*, she thought, *it's too late.*

"Elijah," she said. "It's over. We won. Elijah ..."

Her eyes felt droopy and she thought she might cry again when she heard a voice in her ear. "Did you get 'em back for me?"

Zya looked down to see her friend open his eyes, and she threw her head back in laughter.

CHAPTER TWENTY

To the Victor Go the Spoils

Back on the Nimrod, the Guardians feasted on whatever their minds could conjure. To the thoroughly famished teens, the conference table — filled with burgers, pizza, cheesecake and, of course, Zya's mom's famous fried chicken — seemed like an oasis. The adventure was so thrilling they hadn't even realized how exhausted they were until they got back and immediately passed out. Elijah was the first to wake and got the tour he'd been promised. Kelven patiently answered every question he had, which was perfectly empowering for Eli and utterly exhausting for the Lumerian. By the time they were done, Zya was already eating at the boardroom table, and he was desperate to satisfy his hunger, as well. This was a particularly special treat. Anything they wanted, they could speak into existence.

"Classic Banana Split," Elijah said, and a dish of ice cream instantly materialized.

Zya laughed. "Banana Split?"

"Three scoops of Neapolitan, two banana halves, topped with chocolate sauce, whipped cream and a Maraschino cherry," he said. "Or, as I like to call it ... Heaven in My Mouth."

"How old *are* you?" she asked, wrinkling her nose.

Elijah shrugged, as he loaded a spoonful into his mouth. "Go ahead, hate on a *bonafide classic*," he said. "More for me."

Zya took a bite of her cheeseburger and Eli grabbed one of her mom's drumsticks. He tore off a big bite and his eyes lit up.

"I can't believe you've been hiding this from me," he said between bites. "All this time."

Zya laughed. "I haven't been hiding anything."

And, then, she thought about it. *Had he really never had her mom's fried chicken? Was she hiding something?* She realized that, in all these years, they almost always saw each other at school or in the woods. Otherwise, she went to his place a lot. It certainly hadn't been conscious, or calculated. Maybe, deep down, she just wanted to keep something for herself. But, now that she thought about it, it didn't make any sense that she'd kept home from the only person in the world who *got* her like that. She watched him rip off another bite of drumstick, and smiled.

"Well," she said. "You should come over for dinner soon … maybe Friday?"

He smirked. She loved that mischievous smirk, as if he was about to tell a secret.

"Yeah, I'd love to come over," he said. "As long as your mom's makin' fried chicken."

Zya frowned and smacked him, harmlessly, on the arm. Then, she smiled. "I'll put in a good word."

Just then, the pressurized door slid open and Maroun walked in, followed by his first mate.

"Are you two—Are you feeling yourself again?" Maroun asked.

"I think it's gonna take a couple more milkshakes," Zya cracked, taking a big slurp of her double-thick chocolate malt, as Elijah spooned a slice of ice cream and banana into his.

"Well," Maroun said. "The remaining Archons have evacuated so, at least for now, they're all gone."

"And, what about Enki?" Zya asked.

"We haven't found a trace of him," Maroun replied. "We'll continue to monitor the planet but it's unlikely he survived the amount of energy we measured in that blast."

For some reason, even though the words should have been assuring, Zya felt uneasy. Like the battle was only beginning.

"We'll stay for a fortnight or two and provide assistance as the Earthlings take back charge of their planet," Maroun declared. "You should be proud of yourselves."

Kelven added. "Just let us know when you're ready, and we can send you back."

Elijah paused mid-bite. "We've been gone for a while. What're we gonna tell our parents?"

"No one will be the wiser," Maroun smiled. "You will go back through the door and return to the exact moment you left."

"Mmmm," Elijah nodded. "Typical."

"Will anything have changed?" Zya asked.

"Most likely not," Maroun started.

"*Most likely?*"

"There may be small changes. Things you'd absolutely swear you remember one way might be slightly different — a name, a place, a person. But, if you're worried about disappearing, or your parents never being born, that's not quite how this works. See, time is not linear, as you conceive of it. There are many dimensions, so when we travel backwards or forwards, we are almost certainly traveling to different versions of reality, but never exactly our own."

"Though, even then, the dimensions would have *some* kind of effect on each other," Elijah mused.

"Indeed," Maroun replied. "Whether a dimension is thriving or sliding into chaos, the effect of that ripples out. Change enough dimensions in one direction or the other, and that's when you could see big changes."

"So, what you're saying," Zya interjected, "is that our parents won't magically disappear unless everything turns to shit."

Maroun raised an eyebrow. "That is certainly *one* way you could put it."

The Lumerian pulled a device the size of a quarter out of his robes and handed it to Zya. It was a flat, round disk, much like the battery for an old digital watch. She ran her fingers over the smooth face and turned it over in her hands.

"If you ever need to contact us, use this," he said. "No matter where we are, it will reach us."

"And if you need us?" she asked.

"You'll know."

"Well, we already have our watches," Elijah said, as he licked his spoon clean.

Kelven made a face. "Actually, young sir, we're going to have to ask for those back."

"You don't trust us." Zya said dryly.

"That's not it," Maroun said. "You are Guardians now and forever, but you simply cannot take your power back with you."

"Why not?" Zya asked.

"Some rules are meant to protect everyone," he answered.

As Zya opened her mouth to protest, Maroun added, "But that's all about that for now. We'll let you know when we need you next."

Zya didn't like it. *Not one bit.* But this wasn't a battle worth waging and, as long as nothing bad happened, she was happy to play by the rules. Besides, there would be another adventure soon. She was sure of it. Zya unfastened the watch strap, as did Elijah, and the Guardians handed their pieces over to Kelven.

"Ready?" she asked, looking over at Elijah.

"Ready," he said.

Maroun looked surprised. "Are you sure? You may stay for as long as you like."

Zya looked at Elijah, who nodded as he popped the cherry in his mouth.

"Time stands still for no one."

They followed the Lumerians back to the transporter room and Kelven, working at the console, opened up another portal. Zya's mind flashed back to the beginning of their adventure — when she'd first laid eyes on that magic door in the woods — and she smiled. *You done good, kid*, she told herself. As they stepped up to the portal, Maroun raised his right hand, palm facing out, fingers together, in what appeared to be a gesture of respect.

"Live kindly and be well, Guardians," he said. "And always be ready — you never know when you'll be needed."

Zya and Elijah returned the gesture and, holding hands, stepped through the glowing frame. There was a bright flash and, less than a second later, the two children were standing on the very same patch of forest, in the very same grove of trees, where they'd first stepped through the glowing door. But the portal was no longer there. It was just the two of them, hand in hand, as the low light of dusk tossed a thin veil of darkness over the scene. Using her pointer finger, Zya wiped a glob of chocolate syrup off Elijah's lower lip and, giving it a good stare, licked the finger clean.

"Maybe I'll try one next time," she said, and they both laughed.

"I thought I lost you there for a second," she said, holding his hand in hers.

"Not quite," he winked. "Thanks to you."

They hugged, did their secret handshake and walked back to the edge of the woods, better friends than they'd ever been, and anyone would ever know.

"See you tomorrow morning!" Elijah yelled as he jogged off.

Zya ran home too. She especially loved feeling the wind against her face. With every step, she left the past in her wake. It made her feel powerful to know that, any time she needed to go, her feet could take her there. So, she ran, and ran, and ran. And, by the time Zya spotted the house, she'd broken a light sweat. Only a single sliver of light was left on the horizon, and it disappeared completely as she climbed back up the trellis, slid in through her second story window and closed it shut behind her.

CHAPTER TWENTY-ONE

The Best Is Yet to Come

A maroon Subaru station wagon pulled to a stop in front of George Washington Carver Magnet School. The sidewalk was abuzz as middle and high school students piled out of their parents' cars, swarming to say hi to old friends as they all streamed in through the double front doors. A few of the popular girls congregated next to the main entrance, shifting poses and making judgy faces, as packs of chatting students passed them by. The back door of the station wagon opened and Zya slid out, her signature canvas high-tops hitting the pavement with a smack. She pulled her backpack out behind her and put it on over the same bomber jacket and beanie she wore the night before. She felt lucky with them on, like she was a little more herself.

The front window rolled down and Antonio leaned over. "Hey kid."

She stopped and looked over her shoulder.

"Have a great day," he smiled.

Zya plastered a half-hearted grin across her face and gave an exaggerated thumbs-up. It worked. He rolled the window up and pulled away just as she mounted the stairs. As she passed through the main doors, Zya wrung her wrist. It felt strange without the timepiece. She wanted that version of her back. You know, the "her" that had the power to make things right. And she wondered if it was the watch that made her that way, or if she could find it all on her own.

She walked, unbothered, into a wide hallway that bustled with students, and teachers, carrying binders and books. Everyone was there, grouped into their little cliques, just as she'd imagined. Except, when she imagined it, she'd felt self-conscious and, right now, she didn't care what anyone thought. To her left were the goths. Behind them, a group of nerds crowded around, gawking at the newest edition of their favorite graphic novel. And, on the opposite side, the preps and jocks all kind of blended together. Finally, gathered loosely at the end of the hall were all the debate, theater, math and bus kids.

A golden wisp of color caught Zya's eye, and she turned to see Wendy Werner strut through the doors and down the middle of the hallway. Wendy, a freshman, who already seemed to be head of the girl-boss contingent, breezed past Zya with her brightly colored nails, lip gloss, and designer heels, all paid for by her rich daddy. Everyone knew Wendy was a spoiled brat. Her white crop top even said so, in bright pink jewels. Everything she wore was a statement, including her short, bleached jean skirt. All the heads turned as she strutted by. Not even the comic book nerds were immune.

It all happened so fast. First, a single sheet of white paper floated out from the crowd, landing directly in Wendy's path. Then, out of nowhere, Elijah's head popped out of the crowd as he bent down to pick up the eight-and-a-half by eleven. But he didn't see Wendy and she didn't see him. *Oh no*, Zya thought. *If only I had my watch*. But, before she could intervene, Wendy, who, let's be honest, never really bothered to look where she was walking anyway, tripped over Elijah and slid, all topsy turvy, over the slick hallway floor, landing upside-down in a crowd of unsuspecting eighth graders. Already embarrassed, Wendy scrambled back to her feet. But, during her fall, that short jean skirt had scrunched up around her waist, revealing a pair of white, frilly Hello Kitty underpants.

It was one of the eighth graders who pointed and laughed first. And, then, it was everyone, laughing, and laughing, at the most popular girl in school. She blushed. Wendy had so many victims over the years it was hard to keep track and some of them, no doubt, took pleasure in her embarrassment. Before long, Wendy's girls rallied to her side and, creating a ring of privacy, shielded her from the crowd as she shimmied her skirt back into place. The force of the impact had knocked Elijah on his back, and Zya was helping him up when Wendy, having regained her footing and dignity, glared at him with a fiery passion.

"What are you doing, *bottom feeder*?" she spit out, cheeks flushed. "I was *walking* there."

Zya glared back at the prissy primadonna, as Elijah dusted himself off. "Why don't you put a little more makeup on, Wendy," Zya said. "Your ugly is showing."

The crowd of onlookers reacted raucously, with "Ooohs" and "Ahhhs", and then went totally silent, as they waited for her reply.

"I don't even know who you are, *little girl*," Wendy sneered.

The dig was meant to be malicious, to elicit a reaction, to knock her off her mark, and Zya knew it. The crowd booed at the lazy insult and Zya proudly stood her ground. She wasn't going to back down now. Besides, Wendy wasn't *that* scary anyhow, not after what she dealt with the night before. The whole school watched in rapt silence as Zya took a deep breath and stepped forward, walking right up to the manicured Barbie. She stopped far enough away so as not to be mistaken as threatening, and yet close enough so Wendy could feel her.

"You don't talk to my friend like that," she said, head held high. "I think you owe him an apology."

"An *apology*?" Wendy rolled her eyes. "*He* should be the one apologizing."

"It was a mistake, Wendy, and you know it," Zya shot back. "Besides, you don't own the hallway."

Zya stared directly into Wendy's eyes, and there was a long, drawn out silence, as the girls sized each other up. Then, all of a sudden, Wendy's lip quivered and, with a petulant cry, she turned on her heel and stormed off down the hallway, her minions scrambling to keep up. Zya turned to Elijah and looked at him admonishingly, as the hallway chatter resumed.

"I know," he said. "*I know*."

"You alright?" she asked, as they walked to homeroom.

Elijah clutched his face, looked at his hands and anxiously raised his t-shirt to check his stomach.

"No scales, and not a scratch on me," he said with a clever smirk. "Oh, and, by the way ... thanks."

Zya cracked a smile and playfully elbowed him in the ribs before threading her arm through his.

"Any time."

About the Author

Jabril Yousef Faraj is an award-winning Young Adult Fantasy author. Born in Los Angeles and raised in the Midwest, the nonbinary, Arab-American artist is an Edward R. Murrow award recipient and alumnus of Northwestern's Medill School of Journalism.

Their fiction debut, *Guardians of the Cosmic Clocks: The Emerald Tablets*, won the 2025 Literary Global Children's Book Award for Best Young Adult Novel, was a finalist for the Children's Book International Award in Fantasy, and runner-up at the New York Book Festival. The second book in the series, *Guardians of the Cosmic Clocks: Wings of the Gods*, has earned international recognition.

A homeschooled church kid raised on Nancy Drew, *The Chronicles of Narnia*, and *Reading Rainbow*, Jabril writes to inspire the next generation with imaginative worlds, dynamic characters and a stubborn belief that the pen is still mightier than the sword.

Independently published and promoted through word-of-mouth, we rely on the passion of our readers. If you enjoyed this story, please post your review on Amazon, Goodreads and BarnesandNoble.com so other curious readers can discover *Guardians* for themselves. Join our mailing list, become a patron and contact us by visiting our official website, guardiansofthecosmicclocks.com.